# STREET LIGHT BOLERO

# STREET LIGHT BOLERO

## Michael Paul Hogan

SHANTI ARTS PUBLISHING
BRUNSWICK, MAINE

## Street Light Bolero

Published by Shanti Arts Publishing

Original cover image by Victoria Merki

Shanti Arts LLC
193 Hillside Road
Brunswick, Maine 04011
shantiarts.com

Printed in the United States of America

ISBN: 978-1-962082-52-5 (softcover)

LCCN: 2025934980

*for Susan*

# Contents

# Acknowledgments

Acknowledgements are due to the editors of the following magazines in which the majority of these stories originally appeared:

*Adelaide Literary Magazine*
*Big Bridge*
*BlazeVOX*
*The Blue Nib*
*Cape Magazine*
*Culture Cult Magazine*
*East Lit*
*The Magnolia Review*
*The Oddville Press*
*Peacock Journal*
*New Critique*
*Night Picnic*
*Scryptic*
*Streetlight*
*Synchronized Chaos*

The story "The Fishermen of Dragon-Tooth Beach" has been recorded and can be heard in the archive of the audio-magazine *No Extra Words*.

*Sometimes we have no choice but to dance a bolero under a street light or a red moon.*

— Roberto Bolaño

# Bangka Island Story

There were nine bottles of Bintang beer on the shelf behind the counter of Abdu Rama's beachfront banana shack. On the counter itself there was a watermelon, sliced, in a bowl of ice, and beside the watermelon there was a basket woven out of banana leaves containing a bunch of eight or ten or twelve bananas, all lying on their backs and basking in the sun like the gila seksi foreign ladies on Amerika Serikat TV. Below the counter there was a hand-painted advertisement for Coca-Cola, the paint faded to a pale imitation of red, the raw wood showing through the familiar looping white letters, and in front of the counter there was a three-legged wooden stool upon which Abdu Rama would sit and wait for customers, all the while smoking kretek cigarettes and gazing out at the South China Sea.

•

Weni Nelayanputri was fourteen years old and lived with her grandmother in a two-room house that her father had built before he was lost at sea. She remembered the two days and two nights of vigil at the water's edge, framed through the window of the room in which she and her grandmother slept. And then on the third day there was the truth of what the fishermen said—that disaster is an empty boat. They hauled the boat by lamplight and torch-light to where the palm trees began beside the two-room house that her father had built before he was lost at sea. And from which, only six months later, her mother had also fled, taking the passenger ferry up the Musi River to Palembang, there to drink whiskey and smoke cigarettes and bercinta laki-laki asing to be lost, hilang, in a sea of her own drowning.

She left behind a handbag containing nearly nothing: an empty lipstick and a Hello Kitty hair-slide and a couple of one-hundred-rupiah coins. She also abandoned a red dress that Weni's grandmother had been washing at the time and which Weni now wore, very proud, very seksi, Coca-Cola red, as she walked along the beach to the Saturday market that sold rice and vegetables and chickens and fruit and birds in cages and mermaids that wept for the sea.

・

"Selamat pagi!"

"Pagi, tuan Abdu!"

"Anda ingin Coca-Cola hari ini? Es dingan!"

"Tidak, tuan. Mungkin besok."

"Okay. Selamat jalan, anak."

"Selamat tinggal, tuan Abdu. Terima kasih!"

"Kembali!"

You're welcome! Abdu Rama waved at Weni Nelayanputri and then reassembled his pose on the three-legged stool, the stool upon which he would wait for customers, all the while smoking kretek cigarettes and gazing out at the South China Sea.

・

Exactly ten years ago. The silence then the noise, the silence/noise of a keel being dragged across tide-hardened sand; the flames of the torches and the beams of the lamps reflected off the blades of the machetes and the leaves of the banana trees. They say,

"Bencana adalah perahu kosong,"

It means: "Disaster is an empty boat."

and afterwards they move like shadows between the firelight and the trees,

"Datang pergi, Weni. Come away."

and glance in through unglazed windows at where four-year-old girls and their grandmothers illuminate the darkness with the fear in their eyes.

・

"Hati-hati! Be careful, child. Your feet will menjadi hitam. Turn black!"

The road to the market ran behind the beach but Weni, in defiance of her grandmother, preferred to walk along the sand, swinging her sandals by their straps, separated from motorcycles and the very occasional taksi mobil by a screen of banana trees. She almost didn't see the boy until she was past him, glancing back at a movement that caught the corner of her eye. He was sitting on the ground under the shade of the trees. He wore a faded blue T-shirt and a pair of khaki shorts. In front of him he had made a mat of banana leaves and on this mat there were nine fish, each about a foot in length, their scales still silvery fresh from the sea, the blood around their gills undried. She looked down at the fish and then back at the boy. His hair was long and fell over his eyes and his smile when he smiled was like a coconut split with a machete. He said,

"Don't be afraid. Aku tidak hantu. I am not a ghost."

He said,

"Buy my fish if you don't believe me. Since when did hantu menjual ikan? Did ghosts sell fish?"

He smiled his smile again. He said,

"My name is Budi Haryanto. I like your red dress."

A motorcycle backfired on the road behind the banana trees and a bird, startled from within the branches, slapped its wings against the leaves. The boy and the girl looked at each other and then, for no apparent reason, merely an act of spontaneous and unaffected friendship, laughed. The girl, Weni Nelayanputri, said,

"We are fishing people. We catch. We do not buy. If my grandmother sends me to the market for rice and I come home with fish . . . "

She hesitated. She said,

"If you give me a fish, I will let you sentuh saya baju merah. Touch my red dress."

She thought she saw a bird in the banana trees but she was mistaken. It was a trick of the sunlight on the leaves. Nothing. The leaves shook briefly. Then became still.

"I will kiss the strap of it where it crosses your shoulder," said the boy, "and I will give you three fish."

Weni had never felt the material of her dress so close to her skin. She said,

"You must close your eyes and keep your hands in the pockets of your celana pendek." And then: "If I allow you. Which I won't."

"I am sincerely sorry," said the boy, Budi Haryanto, "for offending you. But I am in love—"

"Gila! Crazy!"

"—with my fish. All night I catch them wading in the water with a spear and a lantern. Sometimes not even a lantern, just the moon. And all day I sit on the beach and—"

"Oh, oh, you are a beast! A beast and a liar! Binatong dan pembohong! I wouldn't want your fish for a thousand kisses!" And then, unsure if that was correct, she turned on her heels, her bare heels on the shaded sand, slapped her sandals together like castanets, and marched as quickly as was not *too* undignified, the banana leaves rustling with his imagined laughter, mixed up with the real laughter of children on motorcycles, jolting naik dan turun up and down along the potholed road.

Every evening Weni would pour a glass of arak for her grandmother and the two of them would play cards and her grandmother would say,

"Weni, child, you are dreaming. You cannot put a red three on a red nine."

Or:

"Who is this anak laki-laki who steals even the heart from the card you are holding?"

Or:

"Ah-ya! Is it love makes you put a silly jack on nenek's queen?"

But that evening, the evening of the morning Weni came home from the market silent and shy and angry and afraid, her grandmother only said,

"This arak tastes of water. Terbaker kepiting. Like bubbles from a crab's arse. Weni—"

"Nenek?"

"—Tomorrow. Besok. You will go for me along the beach and buy me fish. After *that* you will buy me arak baru. From Abdu Rama. Oh, and Weni child,—"

"Aku tidak mendengarkan. I am not listening"

"—the fish you buy need not be as beautiful as the boy who sells it."

"Nenek! Mengapa anda malu saya? Why do you shame me?"

Weni's grandmother placed a red six on a black five. She said,

"This arak is neither water nor crab's piss, but somewhere peralihan. Meaning in between."

●

"I have a favor to ask you, Abdu tuan."

"I listen."

"Can you tell me if you ever buy fish from a boy who sells beneath the banana trees?"

"That is not a favor, child, that is a question. But the answer is no. Who is so crazy to sell beneath a banana tree? Who is so crazy to buy?"

"It was a foolish question. But a favor I have ... "

Abdu Rama laughed a short dry laugh. He said,

"Yes, child, I know. Your tight-fisted nenek has been buying arak from Dedi Surya who, as everybody in the universe knows, makes it from his own piss then waters it down with the piss of crabs. *Now* she wants Uncle Abdu's five-star gold label satisfaction guaranteed in Amerika Serikat rinsed-out Coca-Cola bottle. True or not true?"

"True, Abdu tuan," said Weni Nelayanputri. She tried not to openly disrespect her grandmother by smiling, although the joke had been a familiar one these many years and she was on the edge of knowing that not smiling made the joke better, not the disrespect less. She said,

"If I meet a boy under a banana tree, what shall I do?"

Abdu Rama took a draw on his cigarette. He said, and his voice had the joke erased from it, as a Coca-Cola sign may be erased by wind and sea, he said,

"If he sits under a banana tree, he is not a boy. You shall walk away, anak sayang, stay fortunate, get not eaten, tidak dimakan, by some ghost who steals an empty boat and sells imaginary fish." He flattened his eyes against the horizon, staying silent for the space of a minute. He said,

"They say disaster is an empty boat. A worse disaster is an empty heart. That is what it truly means to be a ghost."

He seemed about to say more and Weni, her chest filled with something she could not describe, neither fear nor disappointment nor love, but something more than and containing each, felt as though she were underwater, looking up through the surface of the sea. The sky shimmered. The sunlight was shattered like a yellow vase. The keels of the boats were visible, their paintwork rippling blue and red and green. She opened her mouth not to speak but to breath. She said, "Abdu Rama!" and Abdu Rama said,

"Ah, sudahlah! Never mind! Hujan membersihkan daun. The rain cleans the leaves. Daun minum hujan. The leaves drink the rain. Disaster? Tidak ada jenis perahu. Disaster for your nenek is an empty bottle! Tell her I shall bring it personally when the sun is behind the trees. More time for marking the cards she will cheat me with. Weni,—"

"Paman? Tuan?"

"—is he handsome, the boy who pretends to be a ghost, who wishes to make you believe he is more than a man?"

"He is a *real* ghost and that is why he sits under banana trees and pretends to think he can cheat me. He is a fool!"

"Even a ghost can be a fool. They are human in that. Tingkat tertentu kredit. True. Benar. And who is a wise man under a banana tree?"

"I will burn my red dress," said Weni Nelayanputri, ignoring the question, and stamping her heel into the sand, "and sew a new one made of all the black pieces." She said,

"The Coca-Cola can is red and the Coca-Cola inside is black. That is *exactly* the color of my new dress. Gila seksi Amerika. Who can tell me this is not my beach? Abdu Rama tuan,—"

"Weni. Putri."

"—I am to meet a boy with a motorcycle. Who will drive me to the market. Very proud with absence of walking. That is my decision. Who will not care if my feet are black like Coca-Cola, only my heart like a Coca-Cola tin. Oh, and tuan,—"

"I listen because the sea is silent. Carry on."

"—are you happy? Sometimes my nenek asks me. Because I see you every day in the to-and-froing of rice and minyak goreng. Always alone. Always gazing. It seems to me—"

"It seems?"

"—It seems." She hesitated. She said,

"Forgive me, tuan. Tampaknya tidak ada. It seems nothing. In the meantime, I am newly decided! Semua sampah! I shall wear my red dress every day and care nothing for boys. Boys or ghosts or motorcycles. It is not for me to care. But I often wonder—"

"Wonder?"

"—how a boy can be a ghost and still have eyes the color of the sea . . . "

There was a silence the width of a wave and Abdu Rama said,

"I do not know." He examined the tip of his cigarette and flicked the ash with his fingernail. He said: "And am too old to become wiser than a child."

•

She woke up screaming and the windows were fire. Her nenek said "Calm, calm, child," and the silhouette of her was black against red. The gray of her hair a swish of a brush. She said,

"Stay sleeping, child."

and there were voices, urgent voices, and then shouting somewhere distant, and then the profile of her nenek against the flames outside. She said (Weni said),

"Is my father home now?"

and there was the sound of her mother and the *thwack-sh* of bare heels against impacted sand. And a voice saying,

"Bahkan perahu beruntung!"

and then the silence concentrated in her mother's shoulders. And afterwards nothing merely to remember. Just a different silence. And shapes and shadows and nothing clearly. Like a village in the morning when the storm has been.

"Selamat pagi, tuan Abdu!"

"Selemat jalan!"

Weni Nelayanputri swung her sandals so the heels *slap-clicked* like Spanyol kastanyet. Like Spanish castanets. She said,

"Nenek says: Buy bananas if they are green, not ripe. Oh, and she says also: If Abdu tuan is feeling stupid, meaning bodoh, he can come and lose all his Coca-Cola seksi lazy money playing hati yang mengalahkan." She hesitated. She said, "Abdu tuan—"

"Uh-huh?"

"It is nothing. Oh, but something—"

" ? "

"—I am instructed to tell you that my father's boat is to be painted blue and red and green and made fit with caulk to sail again. Berlayar lagi. Tuan . . . ?"

"I listen."

"Was my mother beautiful?"

Abdu Rama removed the kretek cigarette from his mouth between the two fingers of his hand and held it the way a broken mast is balanced above the sea. He said,

"I have no recollection."

He said,

"Benar-benar. Truly. Aku punya tidak ingat sama sekali."

He used his thumb and his middle finger to snuff the cigarette. He flicked it away. He said,

"In fact, I am lying to you, child. Anak-anak. She was more beautiful. Even than everybody. Even than the sea."

There was a silence. Weni said,

"There is a boy on a motorcycle, tuan, who says I am in my red dress seksi merah cantik wanita."

"He speaks tidak semestinya. Without manners. But not untrue."

"But if he should ask me to let him touch my dress, I will tell him exactly what pipe he should smoke with! Like Nenek says: Ratu pintar; jack konyol. For good measure. Smoke *that!*"

She went down the beach eighty-ninety yards until she was a red triangle between the banana trees and the sea. She turned around. She put one hand either side of her mouth. She said (she shouted),

"And even not a motorcycle unless it's seksi merah Amerika Serikat. Harley Davidson. Johnny Depp ya. Noise like aeroplane! Benar-benar!"

Then she laughed and waved her sandals and disappeared behind an outcrop of the banana trees.

# Paris Vagrant

I often wander through the streets of Paris completely destitute, wearing a corduroy jacket and a workingman's cap, accompanied only by the sound of the nails in the soles of my boots as I clatter and spark beside the quais and under the bridges along the banks of the Seine—although sometimes, from the shadows of an archway, a voice will cry out,

"Bonjour, Monsieur le Vagabond!"

"Bonjour, Jean-Jacques le Chapardeur!"

"Are you come to repay the cigarette I gave you?"

"The cigarette from the cigarette case you stole in the Luxembourg Gardens?"

"The cigarette you *owe* me, you thieving swine."

"The cigarette that burns like a candle in your sister's eye socket? Adieu, mon ami."

"Va au diable!"

"Farewell."

The nights are cold but the dawns are colder. Even the sparks I strike off the cobblestones are as cold as stars. Sometimes a man will approach me, a well-dressed man, a man in a knee-length overcoat and with turn-ups on his well-cut trousers and wearing English-style leather shoes, a man who will congratulate me on my poverty—

"You must be a poet, my son. To be so poor is to understand the passion of Rimbaud and Villon. Do you understand what I mean by the word passion?"

"I think I do, sir. It means suffering."

"To suffer is a gift, my son, a gift you must use as the vagabond poets of the streets used it before you. Here—"

and then put a hundred-Franc note in my dirt-engrained hand.

"Thank you, sir. Thank you!"

I look up from the almost unbelievable piece of paper, but he is gone, his footsteps deadened by the mist that haunts the early morning river, only the echo of his parting phrase

"Je vous en prie! Spend it not wisely, my son, but well!"

hanging in the damp and dismal air like the music of a *bal musette*.

•

I wake up in darkness—not the darkness of night, but the beautiful sub-aquatic darkness of a room from which the sunlight has been filtered through window blinds and green velvet curtains that hang from ceiling to floor. The darkness of safety. Of tranquility. Of caves in the sides of mountains that hide behind waterfalls ...

Of bathyspheres lowered by winches and cables through the depths of the oceans to the bottom of the sea ...

•

"Wake up! Wake up, why won't you?"

The knocking on the door is like physical pain, the anticipation of the next blow worse than the pain of the last—

"Open the door. We know you're in there!"

To open the door would be to die. To open the door would be to let Death enter, a form of suicide, as impossible, as appalling, as truly sickening as the contemplation of a pavement ten / twelve stories below, the crack of one's head on icy concrete, the echo of the shattering of one's skull, the sound of fists on a sanctuary door, the voices goading you to Jump! Jump! Jump!

"Open up, damn you! You know you can't stay in there forever!"

I grind my face into the pillow and clutch the counterpane until my knuckles turn white. I say (but softly, so softly that only a sparrow on a chimney pot in Montmartre can hear),

"Yes, I can! Yes, I can! Yes, I *can* ... "

•

I stand up from the floating platform upon which Scott and Zelda Fitzgerald are lounging behind identical pairs of blue-tinted silver-framed sun spectacles and dive in a perfect arc into the turquoise-lacquered golden-rippled Cap d'Antibes.

•

The captain of the Marie Roget tightened the lid of the bathysphere one last time, saluted us through the thickened glass observation window, and gave orders for Professor Apollinax and myself to be lowered into the deep ...

How extraordinary to descend through strata beneath strata of seemingly infinite varieties of blue then green then previously unknown variations of purple, ending (or merely beginning?) with the profoundest, most psychologically oppressive expression of black! The fish that populate these deeps are of a nature so grotesque to be almost fantastical. They are translucent white and carry their own illumination with which to penetrate the infernal dark. Some have stalks on their heads that carry electric bulbs like wilting flowers; others are studded with lights and thus resemble illuminated bateaux mouches on the Paris Seine. After thirty or forty minutes of awed silence I turned to Professor Apollinax and said,

"My dear Professor, I do believe we have entered a world of which God is as ignorant as we."

"My earnest fear," replied the Professor, "is that God is ignorant of *our* world and that we have intruded into the world of God ... "

•

I smoke a cigarette in the semi-darkness of my room and pray the silence will continue. Just time, I hear myself asking, just time to drink one more glass of cognac, to smoke one more from a sky-blue packet of Gauloises *caporal*... The smoke hangs in the air, undulating, ululating, rippling the way jellyfish ripple in the South China Sea ...

•

After three hours of continuous descent, during which Professor Apollinax filled an entire notebook with detailed sketches and commentaries, I began to experience an alternative reality in which I was the occupant of a balloon taking off from the Luxembourg Gardens in Paris on a cold (it was cold in the bathysphere) December afternoon. The fish, with their extraordinary lamp-like illuminations, became a circle of photographers, all of whom wore top hats, their flash-bulbs exploding, the puffs of smoke hanging and then dissolving in the chilly air. I waved my handkerchief from the basket, acknowledging the cheers of a small but enthusiastic crowd. The anchors were cut free. I was almost immediately fifty feet above the ground.

How beautiful the roofs of Paris are, seen from their own elevation, dusted with a gorgeous chiaroscuro of soot and snow! I turned up the collar of my overcoat and floated over the *Quartier Latin* of Montparnasse, the windows and skylights of the artists' ateliers flickering silver and yellow in the rapidly darkening late afternoon, an occasional face framed in the anguish of composition as I (and my balloon) floated only a few feet from the grimy slates and silhouetted chimney tops. Hola! In one an artist with his back to me was painting a model who lay naked on a divan. The model was a strikingly beautiful young girl of maybe nineteen, but the portrait on the canvas was an extraordinary collage of seemingly random colors and shapes. As though to see a balloon floating just outside the window was the most natural thing in the world, the girl acknowledged my presence with the merest flicker of a smile, an almost imperceptible enlargement of one eye, both of which I returned with the smallest of bows. A few moments later my gondola bumped against the begrimed and frosty pane of a writer's garret. The writer, his eyes reddened with lack of sleep and excess of absinthe, looked up from his manuscript and assumed such a look of astonishment that I immediately feared for what little might be left of his sanity and was pleased when the balloon drifted up and over the rooftop, its basket dislodging a slate as it gained the comparative freedom of the smoky Paris sky. Thus it was that while Professor Apollinax plunged further down into the depths of the ocean, his voyage illuminated by the lamps of undersea creatures previously unknown to science, I made a mirror-image ascent, my own extraordinary journey lit by the infinite and gorgeous familiarity of the stars . . .

•

I fear the clock. The clock is perfectly round and has two bells that are activated by the minute hand. The clock is black enamel and has a white face printed with twelve numbers that sometimes I cannot understand. The person in an adjacent bed, back *then*, once told me how to stop the minute hand from reaching the point where the nurses and the men with their own clock-white faces rush in. It is as easy, he said, as putting your hand through the mirror. Even your whole body, he said, can pass through a mirror, but to stop the moon from crossing the sky requires years of meditation—meditation which, he went on to confide, he had himself undertaken in the mountains of Shangri La. "There was one occasion," he said, "are you listening, my friend?"

"I'm listening."

"It was on the third night of the Lantern Festival in the ninth lunar month of the year I was reborn as Hu Yue Liang. I said farewell to my teacher, my *laoshi*, and walked out of the temple where I had studied The Way for nine hundred and ninety-nine days. The ice underneath my bare feet was like broken glass—like broken glass, my friend! Are you listening?"

"I'm listening."

"And the moon, the full moon, was as big as—"

"As big as?"

"—as the eye of infinity, my friend, as a black hole filled with the tears of God! And yet as small as a doubloon nailed to the mast of a whaling ship. My feet bled 'til the snow turned crimson, but I felt no pain. No pain at all! It is strange, is it not? that pills so small can make everything stop, even the rain . . . "

But the clock, I'd said, what about the *clock?*

"With a wand made from a feather from the roc that Sinbad slew on his seventh voyage. And, ah, my friend, what extraordinary travels we will have together in search of *that!*"

•

The base of the floating platform ripples in the clear blue water, the faces of Scott and Zelda shimmering into focus above the sunlit surface of the sea. I burst through the dancing golden glimmer and grasp a hand and shake the water out of my eyes and laugh, the water gallooping and galoshing around the sudden unwieldiness of the platform's reinforced base, the hand holding mine and guiding me to the rope handles that effect a leverage up and out of the blue. I'm aware of a girl in a turquoise bathing costume reclining sideways on one elbow, smoking a cigarette in a black and silver holder, beholding me with casual amusement, and then hoisting myself up onto the platform in a slither of hands and knees. Scott pours me a glass of white wine from a bottle of Pouilly Fuisse in an ice bucket and Zelda throws me an enormous blue and white towel embroidered with the name of L'Hotel du Cap. The girl in the turquoise bathing suit continues to study me for maybe thirty seconds then casually turns away.

•

I must have slept. I opened my eyes and was momentarily disorientated. It was nothing but natural to transpose my confusion to my companion. I said,

"Are you alright, Professor Apollinax?"

His eyes twinkled behind his spectacles. Instead of twinkled I might have said radiated. When he spoke his voice positively burbled with excitement—excitement he was at very few pains to suppress. He said,

"Alright? You ask me if I am alright? Ah, my dear young fellow, look out of the starboard port and see what I see . . . "

I looked as directed and gradually, through the murk with which, albeit briefly, I had allowed my eyes to become unaccustomed, an extraordinary thing came into focus. I said,

"I see a peculiar creature, professor. And a rather big one too, by all accounts."

Professor Apollinax chuckled and rubbed his hands together over his knees. He said,

"Not merely a creature, nor merely a big one either. Oh, my dear boy, this is the greatest moment of my life—I have seen a living Plesiosaur!"

·

"My *incidents*, as you call them, are nobody's business but my own. Occasionally, I admit, I confine myself in my room, but I forcefully insist that solitude is simultaneously man's greatest freedom and greatest right. That *paradox*, Monsieur le Docteur, is something that, with your pedant's lack of irony, you fail to understand—worse, you fail in every aspect of empathy that, I would most keenly have thought and you should most keenly be aware, is part of the essential, the *quint*essential makeup of the practitioner who seeks access to the intricacies of the human mind. *My* mind, my dear Sigmund *Fraud*, ist ein System von sehnsüchtigen Trugbildern zusammen mit einer Abweisung der Wirklichkeit, wie finden wir nirgends sonst aber in einem Zustand der glücklichen halluzinatorischen Verwirrung. I am insane only to the point at which I act entirely in concordance with the dictates of my own, my original and unique mind. And if every mind is simultaneously unique and discreet then we are either all of us or none of us insane. Ah, Herr Doktor, what do you think of that! Hola! Your silence betrays either a jealousy of superior intellectual capability or a merely inadequate presence of mind. Of mind! Of all the minds in this clinic, only the clocks are insane. And I have a plan to deal with them—indeed! And now if you will excuse me, Monsieur *Froid*, I will accompany my next *incident* with a glass of Jerez and an intimately slender Dutch cigar.

"Would you care to join me?"

## The Incident of the Slate

"Sacre bleu! What on earth was *that?*"

I often wander through the streets of Paris completely destitute, wearing a corduroy jacket and a workingman's cap, accompanied only by the sound of the nails in the soles of my boots as I clatter and spark beside the quais and under the bridges along the banks of the Seine—although sometimes, from the shadows of an archway, a voice will cry out

"Sacre bleu! Faites attention! Attention, monsieur!"

and a slate will pass close enough to my ear to whisper *Hello* before shattering on the cobblestones of the pavement beside me. And across the street the shadow of the gondola of a balloon will darken the chairs and the tables of the Café de Paris, and glancing upwards I will see a face—no, in fact, *two* faces: the face of the otherwise obscure assistant of Professeur Honore de Saint-Sulspice d'Appolinax de l'Academie Francaise, the internationally famous pioneer of submarine exploration, and the pale, emaciated, anxious face of the American poet Edgar Allan Poe, sickened with absinthe and laudanum and the stress of impersonating the bedridden Baudelaire. And then I will look down at the (now shattered) slate and pick up a shard of it and put the shard in my pocket as a souvenir—as a memory, in the literal meaning of the word—and I will touch the rim of my cap to Jean-Jacques le Charpardeur

"Une cigarette, mon ami?"

"Va te faire foutre, vous maudit voleur."

and chuck him a crumpled pack of Gitanes and say,

"Be kind to me, Jean-Jacques. I know how to stop the clocks and the moon. From a man whose feet trod on broken glass."

"You do not impress me with your pitiful charity. Now fuck off and leave me in peace."

"Au revoir. En paix."

"Va tu."

Touching the shard of slate through the corduroy of my jacket pocket, much as a man of superstition might touch a rosary or a rabbit's foot or a medallion of St. Francis—or perhaps even a centime picked up from the puddle of a *pissoir*—I will turn up my collar, tilt my cap to the breeze, and listen to the echo of my own boot-nails as I exhibit my freedom along the white-painted wards of the sanitarium, among the extraordinary creatures of the sub-marine, in chance encounters beside the moonlit ripples of the Seine . . .

# Abdullah
# the Snake Slayer

H is name was Abdullah and he was a slayer of snakes.

•

He lived on the edge of the jungle and beside a river, in a house he had built with his own hands. It was stilted about a foot above the ground and when, during the rains, the river overflowed its banks, the water lapped and rippled around the stilts. For cooking he made a brick oven beside the house, over which he hung a battered kettle, and for his other necessities he used either the river or else walked a few yards into the jungle, behind a screen of bamboo leaves. He lived alone and had always done so. In the evenings he sat on his small veranda, smoking unfiltered kretek cigarettes and listening to the sound of the water and the night frogs and the stars.

On the third day of the rains Abdullah saw a dead snake in the river and recognized it as thé krait he had encountered while squatting behind a banana tree the previous day. Once he had seen a snake he could recognize it again as a man, meeting a former acquaintance after several years on a street in Jakarta, might recognize another man. He watched the dead krait illustrate the pace of the current and blew out a slender plume of kretek smoke.

•

As a young man Abdullah had gone from village to village in South Sumatra, offering his services as a slayer of snakes. Across his back was slung a beautifully oiled and razor-keen machete in a blue and red painted leather scabbard, the blade of which was etched with runes of his own devising. At some villages he was sent away with just a charitable bowl of rice, but in others he was set to work. By the time he was thirty his fame had spread many hundreds of miles. Now, nearing fifty, it was a point of dignity that potential clients came to him. On the seventh day of the rains he looked up from making coffee to see a man approaching from the other side of the river.

This man was riding a donkey. He wore a long white coat, slit behind to the small of his back, that hung down on both sides of him like a bedroom curtain. He wore also a wide-brimmed straw hat that shielded his eyes and from the brim of which dripped the rain. The drops of it clicked like dice on the sleeves of his coat. When he gained the bridge that spanned the river about forty yards above Abdullah's house he dismounted and, leaving the donkey untethered, walked carefully across the slickened bamboo slats. The river now touched the underside of the bridge. Debris, including a broken umbrella, its spokes at strange angles, washed against the upstream side of the bridge. The hem of the man's long white coat rasped against the wet bamboo. Abdullah could hear it from forty yards away where he was making coffee. He went on with its making and waited for the man.

The lid of the kettle lifted and rattled with the pressure of the steam. Using a fisherman's gaff-hook Abdullah removed the kettle from the fire. He placed it on a ceramic tile supported by four bricks and straightened up to receive this man.

The man approached him, holding the hat, now, in a gesture of respect. When he spoke it was in the dialect of that part of the country where rubber plantations surround the village of Beli Tang. Abdullah had killed his first snake there when he was little more than a boy. The man, with self-conscious formality, said,

"Art thou he who is named as Abdullah, Slayer of Snakes?"

Abdullah nodded. He had lived alone too long to desire the necessity of words. With a gesture he led the man to his veranda and bade him sit down. The man seemed suddenly very old and very tired, although Abdullah guessed him to be at least ten years younger than himself. He, the man, removed one hand from his hat brim to brush a bead of rain off his nose. The hand trembled. Abdullah offered him coffee in a tin cup and squatted with his back against the wall. He lit a cigarette. Beads of rain still fell from the man's hat brim. Abdullah heard them shatter when they hit the floor.

A bird screeched from behind the banana trees. The river rippled against the bridge. The man took a deep breath and, speaking, spoke:

"Seven days ago," he said, "my daughter was bitten by a cobra. On the evening of that same day, she died. First, she became paralyzed. Then she turned blind."

He looked past Abdullah at the gray-green shapes of the coconut trees beyond.

"She was ten years old. My wife and I had waited seven patient years to be blessed with a child."

Abdullah shifted his weight and exhaled a coil of kretek smoke. He studied the man as he would a python wrapped around a latrine.

"For three days I hunted through the fields. I took a machete and went every place we warn the children not to go. On the second day, God forgive me, I cursed Allah. On the third day, I cursed myself. I encountered kampung snakes and water snakes and banana snakes and I killed them all. But I never saw a cobra. And I never saw the cobra that ruined my beautiful girl."

There were tears in his eyes and, embarrassed for him, Abdullah shifted his gaze towards the copper-colored stream. He remembered the krait he had seen in the water four days previously, and felt a sudden rush of pity for this man.

"Then," the man continued, "then I remembered. I remembered a man they call Abdullah. Abdullah, the slayer of snakes. They say this man can even speak with snakes. That you can hear the rubber dripping from a rubber tree ten miles away. That you know every cobra in every village by name. And that they respect you. It is also said," and he glanced at Abdullah shyly, as though afraid he might offend, "that on still nights you can even hear the stars."

Abdullah examined the glowing end of his cigarette and nodded.

"They click," he said, "like cicadas at harvest time. But," and he allowed himself a slender smile, "I do not understand their language or what they say."

A wad of still-glowing ash from the end of Abdullah's unfiltered cigarette fell down and hissed on the ceramic floor. The man started. And in that one reaction betrayed the strain of seven sleepless nights and sleepless days. Abdullah felt another wave of pity for this man, as of a breeze that comes up suddenly and ripples the banana leaves. The man fumbled underneath his coat and took from the pocket of his shirt two very shiny orange and green banknotes and offered them to Abdullah. He said, "This is two hundred-thousand rupiah. It is all the money we, my wife and I, our respective families, could raise. We weep for justice, but we are poor. Come back with me to my village, Oh Abdullah. Thou who art Abdullah Akbar, Slayer of Snakes. Kill the cobra that killed my daughter. Then it is done."

How long did it take him to ride here, wondered Abdullah. On that broken-down animal, at least two days. Two days minimum, maybe three. He suddenly realized that the unfiltered cigarette was burning too close to his lips and flicked what was left of it into the mud-stained river. He looked directly at the man.

"You are too late," he said. "The cobra that killed your daughter is already dead."

The man's face was a dirty white, like a much-handled disc of tailor's chalk. He said,

"What are you saying to me?"

"Only this. I met the snake that killed your daughter four days ago. It had been attacked by an eagle. It confessed the murder of your daughter and then I chopped off its head. It was already half-dead when I killed him. Half the fee is sufficient. I return the rest. The story is done."

And then, finally, at last, the man whose donkey still stood patiently on the far side of the river, the coat of whom made a wet semi-circle around him on the ceramic floor, allowed himself the expulsion of grief. He put his face in his hands and cried; cried louder even than the river that shattered its debris against the underside of the bridge. And Abdullah stood up and moved himself discreetly behind where he went to be private behind where the jungle started and allowed this man the privacy of his grief.

"Allahu Akbar," he said to himself, but nearly out loud, "Abdullah Akbar. Abdullah is only a man. A cobra is only a cobra. Allah is great."

•

Thirty minutes later the man re-crossed the bridge, remounted the donkey, and, with a tip of his hat, rode away towards where the sky was preparing an evening of endless rain. He was silhouetted for just a few minutes before he disappeared into the banana groves. Abdullah watched him away. Then he returned to his house, the house he had built with his own hands, and went into the room that was made for sleeping. On the wall, hung from a nail, there was a machete in a leather scabbard and, without touching the scabbard itself, he removed the machete, still well-oiled and smoothly capable, running out of its sheath as silently as perfectly as a man might remove himself from a woman with whom he has just finished the beginning of a child. Its blade was as sharp as the moon. Satisfied, he re-sheathed it and lay down on the banana box pallet that was his bed. Tomorrow, at dawn, he needed to take a bus to the village of Beli Tang, there a cobra to kill. But in the meantime, he lay down and closed his eyes.

And listened to the stars.

# Forgotten Young Men on the Literary Trapeze

C harles Jackson once walked into a pawn shop on Second Avenue wearing a double-breasted blue suit with a narrow chalk-stripe and carrying a Remington portable typewriter in a black wooden case. A bell over the door rang when he entered and a bird in a cage hanging from an old-fashioned hat stand made the sound that plastic window blinds make when a cop tries to strike a match on them to light a cigarette. There was a fake-fur coat hanging from another arm of the hat stand and in the left-hand pocket of the coat there was a stick bomb from World War One and in the right-hand pocket a wooden ruler marked in inches and centimeters. From behind a glass-topped counter a surprisingly well-made, surprisingly good-looking young man glanced up at the sound of bird and bell, a jeweler's lens still screwed like a light-bulb into the socket of his left eye, a silk handkerchief flopping lazily from the breast pocket of his shirt. An instantaneous *frisson* of acknowledgment passed between them. The button-sized rubber beads on the base of the typewriter case made a small window-leather scream against the surface of the glass counter. The bird rattled its beak against the bars of its cage. The pawn broker's son or nephew or assistant or whoever he was said,

"It needs a new ribbon. Most folks don't know how to change 'em. Twenty dollars. Best I can do."

Figure it's a bright November day with just a hint in the air of snow; the sort of thin snow that kind of whirls around but never lands on anything. What my grandmother used to call "miser's snow." Charles Jackson put his hands in his pants pockets, *scrunched* them down, and thirty minutes later was sitting at the counter of a bar on Fifty-third and Fifth. The bartender put down a double scotch and a glass of beer and went back to polishing the bottles on a mirror-backed shelf. Charles Jackson took a mouthful of the beer and then out of the pocket of the jacket of his double-breasted blue suit with a narrow chalk-stripe he took a cardboard pill box and out of the cardboard pill box he took two Seconal and the two Seconal he swallowed down with another two mouthfuls of the beer. Then bedded them in with a twist of scotch. The bartender took down a bottle, polished it, and put it back. Took down the next. Charles Jackson, feeling everything take nice effect, loosened his tie and pushed back the brim of his hat. Did I forget to tell you he wore a hat? Of course, he did! This was New York in 1934, take a look at the movies, take a look at the photographs, *everybody* wore a hat—even

Clark Gable in *It Happened One Night.* Even everybody on the Greyhound bus where they sing

> *He swings through the air with the greatest of ease,*
> *That daring young man on the flying trapeze* . . .

Hats were *total.* So Charles Jackson set his hat back of his head and drank the scotch and ordered another and loosened his tie a little looser and ordered a third. After the third, by a process of logical mathematical progression, there must be a fourth—but *that* isn't what was important right there and then. If you looked at the way the all the labels on the bottles were reflecting / flected, and the parallels and camera-angles on the shelfs the shelfs descending, tilting, escalating, wasn't it that, dammit, *that!* that if you wrote would be it more terrific even Hemingway more than better truly *truly* way, oh yes oh gorgeous yes! far *out* and everybody would most definitely def, "Hey, soldier!"

A muscle twitched above the bartender's shoulder blade, the shoulder blade of the shoulder of the arm holding a bottle of Chivas Regal up to the light. He glanced in the mirror at the guy at the bar and replaced the bottle on the shelf. He came forward, wiping his hands on the polishing cloth. He said,

"Uh, huh?"

"Did you ever read *The Three Day Blow*?"

"Can't say I did, sir." Then: "If it's about boxing, I prefer the track."

"It's about—*everything*," said Charles Jackson. And suddenly he had the awfullest, damnedest feeling he was about to cry. He took a handkerchief out of his pants pocket and made like he was dabbing at a fleck of grit in the corner of his eye. A pawnbroker's ticket for a Remington Portable No. 5 typewriter came out of his pocket along with the handkerchief and floated down unnoticed onto the beer-stained wooden floor. He said, Charles Jackson said,

"I think, if you don't mind, and under the circumstances, I will have another glass of whiskey and, if convenience permits, an also glass of beer."

•

If 1934 wasn't the *best* of all possible years for Charles Jackson, it was certainly a good year for another, a very *different* writer, for it was the year that William Saroyan's breakthrough story "The Daring Young Man on the Flying Trapeze" was published in (appropriately) *Story* magazine.

Meanwhile, a whole bunch of other writers destined to be famous in the 'forties were pursuing the agendas that would see them get there. Businessman Frederic Wakeman had taken his family over to Cuba or Bermuda or wherever it was—somewhere nearly-but-not-quite America—and was twelve years away from *The Hucksters*, while Mary Jane Ward was experimenting with short stories in Greenwich Village, likewise twelve years away from her own masterpiece, *The Snake Pit*, based on her subsequent breakdown and incarceration in Rockland State Hospital, a mental institution in Orangeburg, New York. As for Charles Jackson—well, he himself had exactly ten years to go before the publication of his (indeed, America's) alcoholic masterpiece *The Lost Weekend* . . . .

"Set 'em up, soldier, and I'll tell you a story Hemingway *didn't* write . . . "

When I lived in Key West twenty-odd years ago I rented the ground floor of a house on Varela Street and balanced my typewriter on a plank of wood across two orange boxes and used a couple more orange boxes to make a set of bookshelves—on the top shelf of which I had first edition copies of all of these books, *The Hucksters, The Snake Pit, The Lost Weekend*, as well as *Best Short Stories of William Saroyan* (1945), the collection that contains my all-time favorite of his, *The Sunday Zeppelin*, plus about a dozen more almost equally good. I'd picked them up from the bargain boxes of Key West second-hand bookstores for a dollar or two apiece—*first editions! A dollar or two!*—and read them with the sheer joy of discovery, for nobody, absolutely nobody, nobody *else*, read them then (or reads them now), and so there was, there had been, nobody to tell me how brilliant, how totally unexpectedly *great* they were. So I guess basically what I thought was—

Jesus, what a literary trapeze this business is! And falling off has *nothing* to do with your hands with your talent with your timing with your practice with your confidence with your audience with *any*thing. It has to do with who catches you or who doesn't catch you. And you can be the best in the world who ever lived, but if the catcher doesn't catch . . . Well, be the best that ever was, be the best of your whole damned gener*ation*, but like I say, if the catcher doesn't catch . . . For*get* it. You can't legislate for *that* . . .

•

"Now you weren't aiming to steal that car, were you?"

The boy stepped back from the black Plymouth sedan with whitewall tires that was parked up at where the road forked down to the landing stage or carried on to the bridge upstream.

"No, sir!"

"Relieved to hear it. Hate to have to steal it back off of you."

The man who'd spoken came out from behind some bushes, still buttoning up the top button of his pants, a biggish man in a black suit with a black vest, his hat pushed back a little on account of the Virginia heat, his shirt collar showing white against all the black. He said,

"Not that it ain't good for much else—except stealing, given it barely got me these eighty miles to—to where, sonny? Where am I ended up at?"

"Nowhere, sir. Only Moundsville. Moundsville, Marshall County." The boy hesitated, he said, "Listen, mister, I wasn't aiming to steal your car. Only admiring it. We don't get many out-of-state automobiles riding through these days, and when we do, they ain't got preachers riding 'em. You *are* a preacher?"

"Smart, boy. And what about you? Smart enough to want to be a preacher yourself?"

"Smart enough to be a painter, sir. Or maybe a writer. But I prefer to paint."

"How old are you, anyhow?"

"Fourteen, sir. Fifteen in July."

"See these hands?"

"I surely do, sir."

"Oil made 'em, oil 'stained 'em. Lord knows, *I* ain't no goddammed preacher! Saw one once, S A T A N tattooed on one hand, J E S U S on t'other. Scared the hell outa me. Scared me *aways* from religion, not toward it. Stick with oil stains. *Morally* cleaner. Son?"

"Yessir?"

"This year of our Lord nineteen hundred and thirty-four. Our Lord? The devil, more like. Kids by the side of the road, near dead from hunger. Menfolks and womenfolks near dead as their kids. If I *were* a preacher, I'd spit in m' own eye. What kind of pictures you paint, son?"

"Landscapes mostly. Birds, trees. Everything along the river. People sometimes. Not so much. You sure you ain't no preacher? You kind of talk like."

"You want to know what I do? Why I pitched up here same's I pitch up nearly everywhere this side 'n' that of the Ohio River? I sell typewriters, son. Specifically, the Remington Portable Number Five. If you ever give up painting for writing, you may own a machine like this someday. Though a word to the wise, give up both and take up fishing. Less time-consuming and more profitable." He took off his hat, he ran his finger around the band, he said, "Recommend a place to eat around here? Nothin' fancy. A mug of coffee? Pork 'n' beans?"

A bird flapped and resettled in the trees that separated the road from the river. The sound was like when a cop strikes a match on plastic window blinds to light a cigarette. The boy said,

"There's Joe's Diner, 'bout half a mile back. You maybe missed it without realizing. Food's good and Joe and my father go away back. Joe's wife makes the best pie in town."

"Joe's it is then. Who shall I say recommended me?"

"Davis, sir. Davis Grubb."

The stranger tipped his hat and swung open the driver's door of the Plymouth. The boy caught a glance of a typewriter on the passenger seat. The door slammed, the driver made a three-point turn, then paused and leaned across to shout through the passenger-side window. He said,

"So long, Davis. Davis Grubb. An' if you ever get to be a writer, remember the first typewriter salesman you ever met."

"I surely will do that." Then: "Enjoy your lunch, sir."

"Aim to. So long."

He set himself back behind the wheel and accelerated in the direction of town. The boy stood watching until the road was just a blur of dust. Then the dust settled and the car was a black speck in a shimmer of sunlight.

Then it was gone.

# Slender Horizon

T he horizon was low and flat and so wide you had to rotate your head to get the width of it. It was as flat as a sheet of lasagne and about the same color. Wade Schuyler crushed the empty beer can and threw it as far as he could throw. Its dented glint gleamed back at him from the dust of the roadside. With his hand on the car's ceiling, he swung himself back behind the steering wheel and slammed the driver's door shut. He looked at the girl making-up in the rear-view mirror. He said,

"Alright?"

"Uh-huh."

"Let's ride."

•

On the writer's desk there was a small electric fan. The fan rippled the sheet of paper in the typewriter. To the left of the typewriter there was an ashtray and a stack of typewritten sheets of paper with the ashtray as a paperweight, and on the left a glass of bourbon and a jar of pencils and a small lacquered tray of ephemeral stuff like paperclips and pencil sharpeners and lucky coins and a razor blade. He hit the keys. *Clack-clack-clack.* The vibrations of the words being made rippled against the plastic window blinds. Down on the street a cop was arresting a man for wearing purple underpants.

•

She finished making her mouth with a tube of carmine and rotated the lipstick back into its brass case. She leaned back between the driver's and the passengers' seats and slid the tube between the zipper-teeth of a vanity case. The rear of the Cadillac was spread with books by William Faulkner and Jim Thompson and Cormac McCarthy. Paper-covered editions, their covers yellowed by desert sunlight and peeling backwards in sardonic smiles. There was a typewriter and a rifle and a box of shells. There was a stuffed bear they'd won at a shooting gallery in Oklahoma. She looked at him sideways. She said,

"Wade?"

"Uh-huh?"

"If you spent less time reading, would we have a baby?"

He moved his mouth around then leaned out the driver's window and spat. A toad hopped out from the shadow cast by the Cadillac's tire. He said,

"Maybe."

•

"I intend to illustrate my lecture on Charles Edward Conder with a series of slides—the projector, please, Miss Primthorpe—beginning with one of his most beautifully painted silk fans *The Romantic Excursion*. If the gentleman at the back could dim the lights ever so slightly, please... A little more... Thank you. Conder emigrated to Australia at an early age and made his reputation with the Whistler-inspired painting *The Beach at Mentone*. But to my mind, it was only when he returned to his native England and joined the fin-de-siecle group of Aubrey Beardsley and Ernest Dowson that his unique talent, his extraordinary facility for painting on silk, truly became apparent... "

•

They drove past two gas stations and two roadside diners before the girl who was the passenger said,

"I fantasize."

"You what?"

"I fantasize. I fantasize a cold beer in a real glass instead of those tins gone warm in the trunk. And a real mirror in a real ladies' room. And a bathroom that ain't squattin' the side of the car you ain't at."

He was concentrated on the road, a cigarette between his lips, a pair of Ray-Bans that reflected yourself back at you, his hair whipping around in the breeze. He said,

"When I went, I went the side you weren't."

"I never said you weren't a gentleman."

"So what, then?"

"Still prefer a ladies' room."

"Mirrors and powder and stuff?"

He took the cigarette out of his mouth and held it between the fingers of his hand that held the steering wheel. He said,

"You'll get it."

•

There was an undercut in the river bank where it turned sharp east about a mile beneath the town. The girl's body had caught in the tree-root tangle where the current turned more sharply than the angle of the flow. The sheriff was standing up on the road and the sheriff's deputy was in a skiff with a boatman called Judd Truman who mostly sold moonshine whiskey, thus making him an ambiguous accessory to the solving of a crime. The sheriff called down,

"Hey, Dewayne, you arrived there yet? Or are you goddamn fuckin' fishin'?"

"We're here, boss."

"Well?"

"Girl's here okay. Looks like her alright. I reckon it's the same girl."

"I'm mighty pleased to know that. Oh, and Dewayne—"

"Uh-huh?"

"—did I or did I not buy you a fuckin' walkie-talkie for your promotion to deputy?"

"I recall you did, sir."

"I didn't quite catch that."

"I RECALL YOU DID, SIR."

"WELL WHY AREN'T YOU FUCKIN' USIN' IT?"

"YOU BORROWED IT, SIR. YOU LEANT IT TO YOUR WIFE."

The sheriff took off his hat and examined the hat-band. It was worn thin in a couple of places and badly sweat-stained and one time, not so long ago, in fact, his wife had said, Doug, why don't you get the county to buy you a new hat. Or if the county's too mean, how 'bout I buy you one myself. For your birthday, or somethin'. And he'd said, There's been seven murders during my time in office, honey, seven, in twenty-three years, one precinct in Chicago has that many on New Year's Eve, and this hat's been present at them all. It's what you might call a lucky sort of hat.

He fanned his face with his hat brim. He leaned as far as he dared over the edge of the drop to the river. He could just see the squared-off end of the skiff. He said,

"Just don't move 'til the coroner gets here. YOU GOT THAT?"

"LOUD AND CLEAR, SIR."

There was a journalist from the local paper making notes on a legal pad. He was sitting sideways on the front seat of a parked-up automobile with the door wide open, his city-style wingtips on the dusty running board. He said,

"ANY COMMENT, SHERIFF?"

The sheriff put his hat back on, adjusted it, and said,

"Fuck you."

•

The roadside diner when they arrived at it was nearly as low as the horizon. A thin place with a slatted roof and a wind vane stark against a flat blue sky. Wade Schuyler's Cadillac that used to be red was pink with all the dust it'd picked up and he parked it level with the skyline and swung the driver's door open and stood out. Everything horizontal except two things vertical—the wind vane and Wade. He leaned back from his waist and untensed his shoulder blades and ran the palm of his right hand over his forehead and through his hair. A combination of sweat and grit. He wiped his hand on the thigh of his jeans and took a cigarette out of the pack in his shirt pocket. He leaned in through the open driver's window. He said,

"Let's freshen up."

•

There were three of us, Michael and Scott and me, we were all bartenders in Key Blanco, same shifts, different bars, and one day we borrowed a car and drove up to Miami Beach across the Seven Mile Bridge and through the rest of the keys. Have you ever been to Miami Beach? Shit, man, it's *awesome!* You roll in, top down, *Oye Mi Canto*, Gloria Estefan and the *right here* (Holy fuck!) Sound Machine on the Chevrolet's dashboard full-volume in-flight chick-magnet CD player, beach on your right, art-deco hotels on your left, women so hot they could start *fires* rollerblading through the lights, a swimwear photo-shoot going on right there between the Ralph Lauren polo shirts and silver-rimmed Ray-Bans, turn into the forecourt of a pink and blue hotel, Michael turns off the ignition, turns sideways, grins, I don't mean grins, I mean *ultra-smiles*, the way I bet he hasn't, *hadn't*, since the first Christmas morning when he was six years old, he says,

"If I am not much mistaken, gentlemen, we have found ourselves a home..."

•

There was an outer door and a screen door and both of them clattered when Wade Schuyler and the girl walked in. The counter was at right-angles to the door and there was a Coca-Cola vending machine on the left. The rest of it all was molded plastic chairs and tables, with some booths at the rear. Beyond the booths there was a sign saying restroom and the girl went there and Wade Schuyler went parallel to the bar.

There were eight stools at the bar and six of them were occupied. The two unoccupied stools were adjacent. It made a convenient gap. Wade walked that far and gained the counter. He said,

"Howdy."

"Howdy, mister."

He was too old, too self-possessed to be an employee. Late forties, maybe, thinning hair, wavy-gray, a touch of Italian, either that or Greek, he stood facing Wade wiping his hands on a white cloth tucked into the waistband of his pants, the proprietor definitely, he said,

"What's it to be?"

"Two beers. As cold as you have 'em." Wade grinned. "Some girls like it hot. My girl's spent the last two hours fantasizing cold."

"Uh-huh." The proprietor dropped the cloth so it swung from his waistband. "Comin' right up."

For the first time Wade Schuyler looked sideways, back in the direction of the door he'd come in by, along the line of faces looking at him along the bar. He nodded, he said,

"How you doin'?"

in a sort of general way rather than to anyone specific. The guy on the next-but-one stool was a midget. About three foot tall. He was wearing a policeman's outfit. He said,

"Is that hot bitch you came in with yours?"

and sucked up a sincere slurp of beer through a straw. Wade Schuyler said,

"Yours to guess, my little friend."

and took for himself one of the two vacant stools. He levered the by now very crumpled cigarette pack out of his shirt pocket and extracted a cigarette and seeing a Zippo lighter on the counter in front of the gentleman on the other side of him said,

"May I?"

and the gentleman nodded and Wade flicked the lid open and sparked up. It had been recently filled and made a flame four inches high. Wade recoiled back and then held the lighter away from himself and leaned toward it respectfully and touched the flame with the tip of his cigarette. He snapped shut the lid of the lighter and put it back on the counter. He said,

"Thank you."

and took a deep draw on the cigarette and washed the smoke down with a swallow of beer.

•

An apartment in Chicago, or maybe New York:

"Turn off the fan, will you, honey. It's makin' a draft."

"I need that draft to dry my nails."

"I said turn it *off*, godammit."

"O-*kay*."

•

"Why'd we leave that place?"

"Because a weirdo midget disrespected you."

"Disrespected how?"

"Enough."

"What kind of weirdo *midget*, more like?"

"Typical, as weirdo midgets go. Dressed as a police officer, drinking Budweiser through a straw."

Wade Schuyler shook a cigarette out of the packet he'd bought from the roadside place they'd stopped at and struck a match. It was like dawn suddenly. He said,

"Forget it, honey. The only excuse for midgets is, they're small."

•

He slapped the side of the TV set in a mock but practiced gesture of brotherly condescension. He said,

"Now I ain't one of them salesmen insults his customers with a downright lie. Plenty folks perfectly happy with German, even Japanese home entertainment consoles, and *We Love Dolores* looks pretty much the same whatever make you buy. But if you aspire to somethin' so out of th' ordinary, so sincerely fan*tas*tic, that scientists at NASA are usin' it to look at pictures of Mars, but still at a price the regular honest and decent and patriotic American family can afford, then I can do no better than recommend . . . "

•

It was starting evening and they needed a gas station—somewhere to spend the night. The sky was salmon pink across the horizon, gorgeous everywhere, with what clouds there were backlit purple and staining the Chinese-silk blue sky. He pulled the Cadillac over and stood with one hand on its elongated fender and with the other aimed his urination away from his patent leather boots. In the rapidly diminishing visibility within the passenger seat the girl did one last attempt at makeup, meaning lipstick, hair, before the sunset crashed against the metal roof and left her pitiful and incomplete before the check-in desk of whatever next motel. She said,

"If we die in some terrible road accident, who will bury us?"

Schuyler Wade looked through the near-side rear-side passenger window, at the books by Faulkner and Thompson and McCarthy, at the portable Corona typewriter, at the hunter's rifle, at the box of cartridges, at the stuffed and smiling fairground teddy bear. He said,

"Everybody we've ever met."

He buttoned his jeans. He kicked some dirt over where he'd soiled the desert. He said,

"Except we've never met nobody owns a shovel. Damn."

•

A face appeared outside the bedroom window, a jack o' lantern slatted into horizontal slices, backlit by the gorgeous watermelon of the near-to-setting Californian sun. It said (the face said),

"What's all the fuckin' fandango, huh?"

"My wife and me, I mean your daughter and me, I mean me an' ..."

"I know who you fuckin' is, an' I know who you is fuckin' fuckin'. I only ask is that you do it somewhat less noisily, you hear?"

"Thank you, Mr. Beauchamp. Thank you, sir. I will do so, sir. Entirely."

"In heaven's name, Lewis, you's my son-in-law, my daughter's ... Hell, you's *entitled* to fuck her. Jus' don' invite the whole goddamn county to listen in on it, huh? Oh, an' Lewis—"

"Mr. Beauchamp. Sir."

"You fuckin' my daughter. Whole county knows you fuckin' my daughter. Ease off a little on the formality. Call me Pa."

•

Schuyler Wade hitched up a slat of the window blind and looked out at what he hadn't seen properly when they checked in at midnight thereabouts. A forecourt, a pair of gas pumps, a hose hooked up to an air-pump for fattening tires, a metal sign swinging from the crossbeam of two poles

ROOMS + EATS + GAS

and beyond that the same horizon, flat as a new-laid road when the roller's been done with it. Schuyler Wade let the slat fall back horizontal with a metallic ripple and looked over at the sheet-strewn bed. The girl was naked, face down, dreaming somewhere far away, maybe Oklahoma, walking through the crowded funfair with the guy she'd just met, wearing a halter-neck top, denim shorts, platform-heeled sandals with crisscross straps, drinking a bottle of Coca-Cola through a pink and blue straw, seeing everything through a pair of sun-spectacles with heart-shaped frames, saying,

"Look!"

and him looking where she looked, at a shelf above a shooting gallery where sat a row of three-foot-high bears. He put down a quarter and picked up the rifle laying on the counter, weighed it briefly, raised it, sighted it, and shot a hole clean through the middle of the five of hearts. The hole was so centered there was neither more nor less of the heart in the middle of the card either side. Like symmetry. He laid down the rifle and said to the girl,

"Which one?"

and she pointed to one of the bears, he didn't care which, you seen one fairground bear you seen them all, and he said to the fellow ran the gallery,

"That one."

and the gallery owner, or at least who the owner had run it for him, a slick oily type, hair which he hadn't much of in a comb-over, one gold tooth flashing above a candy-stripe bow tie, smiled a nasty fake smile, he said,

"Steady on, mister. Them bears is jackpot bears. Have to nail five hearts in a card to win one of them bears."

"Is that so?"

"Five hearts, mister. Still four to go."

and Wade Schuyler said Load her up and took the gun and put a hole through the top left heart dead center, same as the first. Top right, bottom right, bottom left. He pulled the bolt back, opened the breech, and laid the gun back down on the counter. He had an audience by this time, no less than six, maybe eight, he said,

"Okay, folks, range is free."

and there was a muttering, somewhere between awe and jealousy, and a man, overweight, not fat, in a blue suit, loosened tie, said,

"Hell, no, mister. Ain't no shootin' after shootin' like that."

and he looked around at his fellow audience and his fellow audience nodded and said, mouths different but working together like sheep grazing, they said,

"No way, mister, no sirree."

and drifted away to spend their nickels and quarters on hoopla or the freak show or the tunnel of love. Wade Schuyler allowed himself a slender smile and took a cigarette out of the pack in his shirt pocket and struck a match on the stock of the rifle he'd been firing. He said,

"Seems like those four shots cost you at least two dollars."

and flicked the match so it landed on the gallery fellow's lapel. He said,

"Now I'll take me that bear."

•

In the courtyard of The Temple of Heaven in Peking, the daughter of the Celestial Emperor Kang Xi ran her slender fingers over the surface of an ornamental pool contained in a bowl of polished jade. A pair of fantail goldfish zig-zagged through the rippled water, their red and gold scales shimmering in the late-morning sunlight. Like imperial armor being beaten in a forge.

•

Flat wide horizons, with sometimes a level range of hills. They came to a roadside shack selling farm produce, spindly beans, corncobs, sweet potatoes, bunches of radish. There was nothing else in any direction as far as could see. Just a road extending endlessly, like a typewriter ribbon unspooled.

The girl had cleared the back seats and was sleeping like a child sleeps, smiling peacefully despite the awkwardness of how she lay. The rifle and shells were in the trunk and the typewriter was in the floor-well behind the driver's seat and the books had been placed in even piles on the front passenger seat and the bear sat on the books. With the books underneath him the bear was the same height as Wade Schuyler. The window was open and his fur blew a little in the breeze. "We'll stop at the next filling station," said Wade Schuyler to the bear.

•

"I need someone who can innovate. Like a teenager. Who did the vampire ad for Jenny Yang? Jason Chou, right? He did the whole thing on his i-phone, shot the footage, cut it, spliced it . . . Also, what's that drink?"

"Dubonnet?"

"Dubonnet. Rebranded Dubonnet for the Shanghai market totally by accident. How? Realized the label was the *exact* same color as the Jenny Yang shoes. Used it in the same vampire ad. Sales in China went up seven hundred percent. When impossibility collides with reality, innovation is the catalyst that makes a nuclear bomb."

"I'm a great fan of your work, Mr. Long."

"Fans are for keeping the air cool. I prefer to raise the temperature up."

•

The Cadillac was worn thin now, as worn and slender as the horizon it had been driving alongside these past three days. They came upon a derelict house set back from the road about a hundred yards, all but two of the windows broken, the front door hanging aslant and by its bottom hinge. Like a broken wing. Wade Schuyler opened the trunk and took out the rifle and slid back the bolt and loaded a shell. He raised the gun and sighted and in that moment of absolute concentration was aware of nothing except the infinitesimal turning of the world. He pulled the trigger and the bullet took an ax-chop out of the wooden door frame just above the hinge. He loaded again and sighted again and this time the door, separated from the hinge that held it, fell sideways against the other side of the frame and slid down onto the stoop. The girl said,

"Schuyler Wade."

"Uh, huh."

"Can I ride up front now?"

Schuyler Wade stowed the rifle back in the trunk. He closed down the lid and rested his hands on the hot metal. He said,

"Better ask that bear."

•

They made love to the chaos of the city, to the noise of the streets. They threw open the windows of their apartment in anticipation of police car sirens and traffic horns, of hurtling fire trucks and screaming neighbors, of single gunshots and breaking glass. When the noise of the night dropped down to a hum, they put records on a gramophone and turned the volume high. Beethoven, Wagner, the *Symphonie Fantastique*. In the morning, in the milk truck hour, they examined the wounds that had been inflicted in jagged pieces of mirror, retrieved like shards of history from the bathroom floor.

•

They came to a town that had been built for a cowboy movie, a whole street Wyatt Earp era, with authentic frontages and no behinds. Just crude scaffolding to prop the illusions up. There was a saloon and a hotel and a sheriff's office; a hitching post and a water trough. Inside the trough there was just a greenish-brownish scum where the water had been. Wade Schuyler pushed open the double swing doors of the saloon and stood in a latticework of wooden poles and struts. The sun shone through from a perfectly clear blue sky. It was one of the saddest things he'd ever seen.

•

"Oh, look, darling, I've never seen anything so beautiful."

He looked where she was looking. On the road ahead, no more than twenty feet away, a peacock had strolled out from the trees and was standing facing them. With such beautiful deliberation that it might have been rehearsed for the occasion, it fanned out its tail into a gorgeous semi-circle of shimmeringly metallic blue and turquoise and green, all its eyes fixed on the young English couple sitting in the bicycle-drawn rickshaw. It was exactly the tableau one imagined would happen on a trip to the Orient. The peacock maintained the position for exactly as long as was deemed necessary then very calmly, very sedately folded its feathers and walked away.

•

They drove on and saw no more buildings, fake or otherwise, for the next three days. They stopped beside a river that maybe once had been big enough to demarcate a county line and now was a shallow runnel of water running around boulders in the bed. They stripped off their clothes and washed them with a small bar of scented soap that had been in the girl's vanity case and filled up an empty Four Roses bourbon bottle and lifted up the hood and put more water in the car. They laid their clothes on the roof and the hood and dangled items of underwear from the wing-mirrors. With what was left of the soap they washed themselves. They let themselves dry standing up in the no more than ankle-deep water. The girl laughed to see Wade Schuyler naked, face and neck and forearms tanned deep brown, the rest of him white. It was a different naked from the naked of motel rooms. She said,

"I ain't felt like this since standing under front lawn sprinklers when I was a kid. Were you ever a kid, Wade Schuyler?"

She was reflected back at herself twice in the lenses of his Ray-Bans. He grinned. He said,

"Maybe. But mostly I reckon I was born grown."

He kneeled on the beach in an attitude of prayer and put both hands around the shaft of the arrow that had penetrated his chest. A flutter of white shirt snagged on the tip of the arrow, protruding about half an inch out of his back. The grains of sand glittered in the Peruvian sunlight and fizzed like the surface of a glass of wine. It is a myth that all conquistadors were cruel, unlettered men and Don Roderigo Cortez was a certain antidote to that myth, being a lover of literature and an amateur painter of more ability than most. It is a myth also that in one's last moments, all one's past life is almost instantaneously replayed. For some, albeit an extraordinarily fortunate few, they see the future unspool before them like a cotton-reel dropped from a seamstress' hand. Don Roderigo spat out a mouthful of blood and watched it resolve itself into the interior of King Philip IV's court a hundred years hence in 1656. There was a little girl who he knew, without knowing how he knew, was the Infanta Margaret Theresa, and there were ladies-in-waiting about, and there was a man in the far distance drawing aside a drapery, and there was a man closer by holding a paint-brush, and there was a mirror with some people in it and there was a very ugly-looking dwarf. He smiled and tried to say something to the painter in the painting but his mouth filled too much with blood again and he only vomited and obscured the painting entirely. He wanted so desperately to speak to everybody in the painting it had just been his extraordinary privilege to see. Even that discomforting dwarf.

He vomited blood again, and this time the blood he vomited was black. Two men, very short, very slender, entered the beach from the trees. One of the men drew his bow and trained an arrow on the dead man's head. The other reached out his toe and used it to press the tip of the arrow sticking out of the dead man's back.

•

Nights they laid a blanket and Wade's leather jacket down on a piece of desert bed-sized, cleared of stones. Love-spent they lay on their backs and smoked a pair of cigarettes and wondered at the nearness and the multitude and the beauty of the stars. The girl said,

"I wish I knew their names. They do all have names, don't they?"

"Sure." He pointed with his cigarette. He said, "You see those seven, look like a pot with a handle?"

"Uh-huh."

"Well, that's called The Plough. Its real name's Ursa Major. Means the big bear."

"Hey, you hear that, big bear? There's some stars named after you!" Then: "How'd you know all that?"

"Worked one time on an oil rig, Gulf of Mexico. Guy I worked with knew the names of all of 'em. The whole sky."

"What happened to him?"

"He died."

She shivered. She pushed her cigarette butt into the sand her side of the blanket. She said,

"Is it true, by the time we see the stars they might be dead already?"

"Uh-huh."

She thought about it for a moment. She said,

"Sometimes I guess that's true for people too."

•

The ceiling fan had been set at maximum and whirred like a helicopter blade. I swear to god, if the room had been turned upside down, it would've taken off. Brad Shulmann from *The Daily Record* tried to strike a match on the window blind and gave up and chucked the match through the slats and tried the edge of the desk with another match and said, What's the story, Steve? And I said, Triple suicide, what does it look like? And Brad looked and saw the husband propped up against the filing cabinet, most of his brains filed from A—D, and the lover slumped down on the strip of carpet between the desk and the liquor cabinet, and the wife sitting on the chair behind the desk with the gun on the floor beside her and one of her eyeballs stuck to the underside of one of the blades of the ceiling fan, and Brad said, How about we call it Manhattan Love Triangle? And he caught the match on a splinter or something, it flamed up, he tilted his cigarette to the match, he chucked the match in the wastepaper basket, he said, Or, if it offends your sensibility, we could just say they died of old age . . . "

•

On the morning of the third day they came to the edge of the world. Or so it seemed to the girl and Wade Schuyler. There was no horizon left, neither slender nor otherwise, the world just ended and dropped off like it'd been cut with a spade. The sun was a deep bitter red, a perfect circle burning through the thinnest shimmer of haze. They got out of the car, right side, left side, and came around the front of it and stood side-by-side. The girl said,

"Is this what the end of the world looks like, Schuyler Wade?"

"I don't know. I never saw a world end before."

"I won't be scared if you ain't."

"I ain't scared, honey. Just curious, is all. Reckon I need to tell you I love you."

"I loves you too, Wade Schuyler. Schuyler Wade."

Stood there in silence. From where the bear was sitting on the center of the back-seat they were two burnt matchsticks silhouetted against the flawless disc of an enormous crimson star.

# CINZANO

T he silence had lengthened to the point where it was awkward. The young man said,

"Have you noticed? Ours is a Cinzano umbrella, but all the others are for Kronenbourg beer."

Despite herself she turned her shoulders the minimum necessary to ascertain it was true. She thought that if she were in a brighter mood, she might look for some metaphor, but nothing presented itself except the very trivial fact that of the five tables on the terrace of the café, four were shaded by umbrellas advertising Kronenbourg 1664 whereas theirs had on each of its six facets the familiar blue and red diagonal logo of Cinzano vermouth. She then irritated herself by noticing that the molded tin ashtray on their table was painted to sell Gauloises Blonde and irritated herself still further by casting a furtive glance at the ashtray on the next table. She thought, Christ, at this rate I'll be counting red Citroens *versus* blue Citroens in the plaza—*and* betting on the bloody outcome. She said,

"Cinzano's insipid unless you put gin in it." Then: "Please leave your lighter on the table. I hate having to keep asking for it, and you know I left mine in the room."

"Sorry."

"It's alright." She took the lighter, a lighter *she* had bought for him, a gold Cartier engraved with his name and her name and Happy Birthday in between, and lit one of her own Gauloises Caporal cigarettes. She blew out a long deliberate plume of smoke. She said,

"It's a pity we weren't able to see Theresa and David. I know you like them."

"I thought you didn't."

She paused just long enough to give the impression she was considering the structure of her response, not the substance of it. She said,

"I don't dislike them. They're just—" She searched for the simile by glancing again at the ashtray on the next table. She found it and turned to face him very brightly, fully aware that he could see himself reflected twice in the lenses of her Dior sun spectacles, immediately above a pair of beautifully shaped and only slightly exaggerated Lancome lips. She said,

"—like Cinzano, darling, but without the gin."

She smiled. She realized she was still holding the lighter and placed it on the faceted zinc table-top next to the Gauloises Blonde ashtray and exactly between them. He said,

"What the hell—We saw enough of them in Paris." Then, "I'm starving. How about bread and olives and some of that local cheese? And a bottle of the wine you liked yesterday." He leaned back over his shoulder. "Garcon!"

She smoothed the tip of her cigarette around the badly damaged face of the cheap tin ashtray, the ashtray advertising the weaker version of the brand she smoked. She thought, I am at the age where being beautiful is offset against the ability to make it work in my favor. She said,

"If you ask them nicely, they'll put it in a basket for us and we can take it down to the beach."

"You don't mind?"

"Why should I mind?"

"Because—" Because yesterday he had suggested the beach and she had wanted to visit that fourteenth century church with the Byzantine-style frescoes, and the day before, when they *had* gone to the beach, she had worn an enormously wide-brimmed hat and a Balenciaga sort-of-kaftan-thing and had spent four hours in the shade with her back to a rock and her knees drawn up to her chin, obscured to the point of childish anonymity. He laughed. He said,

"Why should you?"

He leaned back over his shoulder again, attempting to catch the waiter's eye, then turned back to face her. His expression was that infuriating (because irresistible) combination of charming helplessness and well-rehearsed charm. He said,

"What's the word for strawberries? I know they have some—over there—and they'd be nice after the cheese."

"Fraises."

"Frez. Frez, frez, *frez*. Garcon!"

"Monsieur?"

"Fromage et olives et vin blanc, s'il vous plait." Each word was precise, chiseled in the space between himself and the waiter as surely as the names on the honors board at a private school. "Oh, et le pain, aussi, et peut-etre les fraises?"

"Oui, c'est possible, monsieur. Madame."

"Merci! Et pour la plage," he glanced at his companion, "s'il vous plait."

"Je comprends, monsieur. Madame."

"Merci!"

He smiled, the young man smiled, a smile of self-satisfaction and relief. He said,

"Let's have another drink while we're waiting. Tell you what—I'll have a glass of that Kronenbourg beer and you can have a Cinzano vermouth and we'll match these stupid umbrellas. Same as yesterday."

"Yesterday?"

"Yesterday, you know, the guy renting out the Vespas laughed because your skirt was the exact same color as your Vespa. And the old woman at the church..."

Her attention wandered to where, at the edge of the terrace, there were steps that led down to the beach. The steps were steep—too steep for many, who preferred to detour a few hundred meters to where a shallower descent led off from the road—but they had the rather beautiful effect of causing the people who used them to either appear or disappear swiftly and almost vertically, rather like elevators or trap doors on a stage. She smiled at the thought. She realigned herself in the lenses of his Ray-Bans. She said,

"A glass of Cinzano under a Cinzano umbrella would be—*lovely*, darling. Let's do!"

# Vanessa Wanita Dicat

The restaurant she got a job at was somewhere between Covent Garden and Leicester Square—you know, one of those typical London streets immediately off popular thoroughfares that always seem to have been hosed down with a sort of grayish-brown effluent that pools between the cracks. They gave her a red-and-white-striped blouse and a black apron with a pocket for waitress-pad and pen and a laminated menu with which to familiarize herself before she started. She smiled at that. She had to stop herself looking the manager in the eye and saying, How long does it take to learn nasi goreng? but instead she glanced at the (rather dirty) linoleum floor of the restaurant and said, Thank you very much, and then walked home. The blouse had a button missing off one of the sleeves and the apron had a sort of a whitish-grayish *bloom* that made it look not very clean. The afternoon before her first shift she sat in the bath with the blouse and the apron hanging over the shower rail. A breeze blew in through the open window. The curtain billowed inwards with the breeze. The light through the curtain made ripples on the ceiling. Like an aquarium. She leaned forward and rested her face on her knees.

•

The aeroplane banked sharply over the South China Sea and a sudden ray of sunshine flooded the cabin with the immediacy of an atomic flash. Vanessa Wanita Dicat inclined her head against the window and, with the side of her face pressed against the lozenge of toughened glass, looked down at the gorgeous expanse of purest blue. Then came in sight the first of the Thousand Islands, and between them many small boats, each possessing the absolute clarity of diamonds sprinkled over a jeweler's baize.

•

She smiled. She said,
    "Saya tidak tidur dengan orang asing."
    and touched with the tip of her finger the bubbles on the surface of her beer.

•

They lived in a one-room flat on the third floor of a converted town house on Manchester Street, with a stove and a washbasin in one corner and a toilet and a bathroom half-way down the stairs. She said,

"Hello, good morning!"

to the elderly Polish gentleman on the second floor and the *very* elderly French lady on the floor below that. She wore a pair of sunglasses and a purple blouse and an olive-green skirt. She felt her skirt swish around her knees as she skipped across the hallway and out onto the street.

•

Her boyfriend was a painter. His name was Robert. His canvases were six feet high and four feet wide. He painted with his back to the window and the canvas facing the windows on the opposite side of the street. His style was abstract portraiture, or else completely abstract. If his inspiration was for portraiture, he positioned Vanessa on a small stool in the middle of the room and recreated her in sweeps and panels of red and green and blue. She focused on the wing-nuts on the framework of the easel and tried not to move. Robert wiped his brushes on the hems of his T-shirts and moved his head side to side. Like a bird, thought Vanessa, when his head appeared from around the side of the painting, Like a parrot or a parakeet or some tropical forest bird. She tried not to smile. Robert was only twenty-three but very serious. After they made love, he looked at the ceiling and frowned while he smoked a joint. Marijuana always made Vanessa giggle. It was a balancing act.

•

She visited Bloomsbury and Knightsbridge and Camden Town. She ran the tips of her fingers along the railings in Notting Hill. Along Kensington Park Road and Colville Terrace she looked through the railings and into people's drawing rooms. She imagined living in a whole house and not just a single room. She imagined how the sofas and arm-chairs would feel against her bare legs. In one drawing room an old man was watching a movie on the TV. She couldn't hear the sound but could clearly see the characters on the screen. She stood there for five or six minutes, her face between two railings, her hands around two other railings either side.

●

"I'd like to buy you a drink."

"Why?"

"Because you're beautiful."

They'd met at an ex-pat bar called Erla's Mexican Cafe in Bandung. She said,

"Thank you." Then: "Are you a painter? You have paint under your fingernails."

He said,

"Are you a model? You have paint on the tops of yours!"

Cepat seperti kilat, she thought. Quick as a flash. Terlalu cepat. Too quick. She smiled. She said,

"Saya tidak tidur dengan orang asing."

He raised his glass and his eyebrows simultaneously. She clinked her glass against his. She said,

"It means, Thank you very much for the beer."

●

She felt her skirt swish around her knees as she skipped across the hallway and out onto the street.

●

"It's not *my* fault if you can't paint. It's not *my* fault. It's not *my* fault if nobody likes you. It's not *my* fault nobody *likes* you. It's not *my* fault. It's not *my* fault. It's not—*aieee* . . . "

The sound of his slap rattled the paint brushes in the jam-jars on the windowsill. Down on the street a car-door slammed. Then a double silence. Then the noise of a fly landing on the glass.

●

"Would you like another beer?"

"No, thank you."

"If you lived with me in London, we could drink wine. We could drink wine every day. All you have in Indonesia is beer and arak. And arak's just disgusting."

She thought: Now you will say that you want to paint me. Inevitable. Like the next line of a bad song. She said,

"Sekarang anda akan mengatakan bahwa anda ingin melukis saya. Tak terelakkan. Seperti baris berikutnya sebuah lagu yang buruk."

He smiled uncertainly. She smiled back. Despite herself she knew that she liked him. He said,

"Maybe while I paint you, you could teach me Indonesian."

She thought, You are young and quite handsome. But mostly you are very young. She said,

"Mungkin." His face was a combination of disappointment and confusion. She smiled. Then she laughed. The laugh surprised herself because it was genuine. She said,

"It means Maybe."

•

She lay on the bed in the half-light of a summer's evening, turning the pages of last month's *Vogue*.

•

Robert was sleeping. She maneuvered herself out of the bed and put on his shirt, the shirt that was lying on the floor, and went to the washstand for a glass of water. It was the middle of the morning and it was raining. The rain made the window like the window in the bathroom. She watched two raindrops run down the pane and then join up just before they met the sill. She drank the water and turned to face the painting that Robert had finished / abandoned during the night. Suddenly it was as though the canvas were a mirror and she saw herself looking out through the great swathes of burnt sienna, viridian and cobalt blue. She put out her hand and touched the surface of the paint. It was nearly dry but still slightly tacky against her fingertips. Behind the paint she could see herself, an exotic creature trapped in the artificial jungle of some mad parody of Regent's Park Zoo. The girl in the mirror of the painting looked imploringly at the girl in the window of No. 28 Manchester Street. She said,

"Aku ingin pulang."

She said,

"I want to go home."

•

They were in Erla's Mexican Café in Bandung. She said,

"Saya tidak tidur dengan orang asing."

He said,

"Do you mind if I kiss you?"

"Tolong, tidak ada di sini! Please, not here! Not in front of everybody. Tidak di depan semua orang."

"Later, then."

She was suddenly conscious of every mark, every stain on the surface of the wooden table. She looked down into her handbag, slung over the arm of her chair, for a cigarette. Not facing him made the answer easier. She said,

"Alright."

·

She fed the ducks in Hyde Park and then walked home past Selfridge's, swinging her jacket over her shoulder and stopping in front of each window, imagining herself as her reflection, living in an enchanted world of Dior and Givenchy and diamonds and rubies. Of telephone kiosks and evening gowns and phosphorous moons and stars. Of everything wonderful. Of genuine love and genuine friendship. Of tinsel and tulle.

·

He had taken to locking her out, to making her stand in the street until some other tenant left or entered the building. And then having to sit at the top of the stairs until he decided to come home. He usually smelled of cigarette smoke and alcohol and some brand of women's perfume that she didn't know the name of, let alone wear. The Polish gentleman looked up at her when he came out of the bathroom. She could see him through the stair rails. He said,

"Is you okay, Miss?"

She managed a smile. She said,

"I'm a silly girl. I forgot my key."

"Maybe your boyfriend come soon to home, yes?"

"Mungkin. Maybe."

The Polish gentleman nodded. He carried a towel in one hand and a sponge bag in the other. He raised the hand that held the sponge bag. She managed another smile. She watched him from underneath the banister go back to his room.

·

She ran her fingers along the paint brushes in the jam jars on the windowsill. She touched with her fingertips the bruise under her left eye.

One day, feeling particularly lonely, she went back to Notting Hill and walked along Kensington Park Road, looking for the window of the elderly gentleman watching TV. She remembered it had been on the left-hand side as she walked towards the tube station, and so on her right-hand side now. The distances seemed different, the road itself shorter, and the house fronts were not the same. She came to where she thought it was and looked through the railings. The ground floor curtains were drawn, even though it was the middle of the day. Next door an unfamiliar dog was peering out of the window, waiting for its owners to come home. Vanessa gripped the railings very hard and rested her cheek against the cold metal and thought that it was not possible to feel more desperately alone.

•

They'd borrowed a motorbike and ridden up to the volcano above Bandung. The last part was too steep for the engine, so one walked while the other rode. They held hands and looked down at the boiling lake of the volcano. Their clothes and hair were damp from the steam and went painfully cold on them before they were even half-way back to the city.

•

"You're not even proper Indonesian. You're bloody Chinese."

She watched two raindrops run down the pane and then join up just before they met the sill. She said,

"Tidak ada di sini. Tidak di depan semua orang." She said,

"I'm a silly girl. I forgot my key."

She looked down at the wonderful freedom of the mid-morning street.

She ran cold water into a paint-stained glass.

•

"Not even Indo. Bloody—"

"Aieee..."

•

The boy's name was Ari. He was fourteen years old. He had been a professional fisherman with his father since he was nine years old and had inherited the boat when his father was diambil oleh hiu. Taken by a shark. He loved his boat the way other boys his age might love a girl and barely spent any daylight hours in the beachfront shack he shared with his mother and grandmother and three unmarried sisters. One day, while reeling in a barracuda that later he would sell to a Jakarta restaurant, he glanced up and saw an aeroplane that had taken off from Soekarno-Hatta Airport. The aeroplane was in the middle of its ascent and banking sharply. Its wing dipped and caught the sun, sending out an atomic flash. Ari winced and instinctively shielded his eyes. The barracuda felt the line slacken. The aeroplane slid through the sky as a fish might slide through the water. The after-image of the sun-flash on its wing shimmered and shimmied in the boy's eye. A sort of mirage.

•

The restaurant was on one of those typical London streets immediately off popular thoroughfares that always seem to have been hosed down with a sort of grayish-brown effluent that pools between the cracks. The afternoon before her first shift she sat in the bath with the blouse and the apron hanging over the shower rail. A breeze blew in through the open window. The curtain billowed inwards with the breeze. The light through the curtain made ripples on the ceiling. Like an aquarium. Like the aquarium in Jakarta she'd been taken to when she was a small girl. She looked up and watched the shapes weaving and undulating on the white plaster of the ceiling and the upper wall. Beads of water ran down the strands of her hair and dripped onto her shoulders. She leaned forward and rested her face on her knees.

# On the Subway between Soho and St Tropez

"All aboard! All aboard now! Have your tickets ready, please!"

I have seen him before, the man in the aisle seat three rows down, drinking a martini through a fountain pen. He is a villain of the truest dye, a trafficker in narcotics, paperweights and prosthetic noses. I have often thought to denounce him to the appropriate committee, but have hesitated due to a combination of indecision, cowardice and inherent sense of tact. "Hail, good sir! Are the anchovies in your murdered wife's eye-sockets healing nicely?" Such pleasantries do little to disguise the deep loathing I have for the prissy little orbs of his purple-tinted *pince-nez*.

"Tickets, please! Tickets, please!"

"Excuse me, sir, have we not met? A pavement café in Vienna—Yes!—the year my grandmother threw herself under a tram. Or was it Prague? You have (if you do not mind me saying) the certain haughty indifference of the Gentile combined with the rather unbecoming Golem-like subservience of the Jew. No, by Jove, it was Baden-Baden! A glass of sherry disguised to look like spa water—each of us taking turns to drink! And how we drank that star-shattered night to celebrate the murder, dismemberment and acid-bath obliteration of our obnoxious relatives. Uncles, aunts; nieces, cousins. But none so depraved nor so deserving of such a fate that we could not shed at least one hypocritical tear. . . . Or am I not now perhaps confusing you with a ruffian of saucy meanderings and vulgar advantages with whom . . . in the Roman Baths . . . Caracalla . . . certain acts of *friendship* often . . . misconstrued . . . We internationalists have so many points of reference, do we not? Allow me to give you back your card and request the return of mine. And if you defenestrate, I will disclaim all knowledge and pull down the blind . . ."

The windows through the tunnel go *flapper-flapper flapper-flapper flapper-flapper flap-flap*, with photographs of the dead facing the living in a perpetual silent scream . . .

The Russian lady (with whom I had had a brief dalliance on Platform 15 at Waterloo) reaches up to the overhead luggage rack in order to retrieve a stuffed penguin that had been given to her great grandfather by the Youssoupoffs at Archangelskoie in 1914. We exchange the briefest of glances that acknowledges (but does not advertise) that potentially embarrassing (but still delectably unforgettable) public intimacy. There are noticeable stitches on the penguin where his stuffing has been replaced. Otherwise, as pre-revolutionary penguins go, he is extremely well preserved.

•

"Passports, please, Mesdames et Messieurs. Have your passports ready, please."

•

"So I say to her, I say, Dolores, I pay for your clothes so I can take them off. This is why I buy them—to remove them. If you want to keep them on, then *you* can pay for 'em. Have you any idea how much it costs to undress you? Excuse me. Conductor? How long 'til we get to St Tropez? Thank you. Where was I? Oh, yeah. And off on a tangent, let me tell you, these designers, no baloney, they may charge you half a zillion for a piece of rag with a zipper down the back, but the zippers, no kidding, undo smoother'n a Chinaman up a panda's ass. Smoother. Dolores knows that. Quality. Wait 'til she sees the outfit I got her for the beach. Hoop-la! Sick banana! Conductor? I'm about ready for that drink now . . . "

•

Two men have got on who are unquestionably *spies*. Not just *spies*, but *agents in the pay of a malign foreign power.* I shall watch them closely over the rim of my potted meat sandwich, all the time endeavoring not to arouse their suspicions . . .

•

"Mind the doors, please! Mind the doors!"

•

"Allow me to introduce myself: I am the Count of Wardour, the Duke of Dean, the Marquis of Windmill & Frith. May I compliment you, sir, on the elegance of your widow. Such stoicism in the face of suffering; such fortitude in the midst of grief. (Although no-one can doubt her severe and genuine shock at your premature passing). A glass of port wine, Madame? If it alleviates by just the merest fraction ... provides even the briefest respite ... And I will vouchsafe to return you to your husband— your humble servant, sir—before the process of decomposition is too unhygienically advanced and renders the carriage a place unfit for a lady of your—availa*bility* ... "

•

I am in two minds. I prevaricate. No, no! Yes, yes! I am undecided, schizophrenic, mad as two hatters, twice mad, two-times sane. *Der Januskopf*, der doppelganger, Jekyll & Hyde. I am Poe's *William Wilson*— or maybe not; I haven't decided yet. And *won't* decide. Ha-ha! See how you like that! (Or don't ... ). But one thing I know for certain sure: The lady in the black veil sleeping on the luggage rack is not (as everyone supposes) the Countess of Zanzibar, but in fact a notorious Albanian jewel thief with a semi-furled umbrella instead of an artificial leg who has nine-times bankrupted the Kingdom of Zog. Or else an accountant with a twitch who lodges with Mrs. Valerian on the Bayswater Road and eats bread & butter pudding with a Masonic brick-laying implement and wipes his mouth on her double-chintz. Or vice-versa. Or maybe both. Or maybe just neither at all ...

•

"Next station, Leicester Square. Change for the Piccadilly Line and St Tropez. Mind the gap!"

•

"Is this seat taken? Of course it is not! Only a fool would suppose ... Do you mind if I ... Ah, there you see ... a centipede crawling up the cushion in a state of ignorant hundred-footed bliss! To have sat down would've been to obliterate the potential buyer of fifty pairs of sturdy walking boots, ballet pumps, ice-skates or (Heaven bless 'em!) Lancastrian mill-workers' clogs. Laymen may think me strange, dear sir, but in certain institutions with sturdy walls I am known as The Cobblers' Friend!"

•

"Mind the gap, now! Mind the gap!"

•

"My dear lady, your arm if I may. The gap between the carriage and the platform has been known to swallow caparisoned elephants ridden by the Maharajahs of Mangalore, whales of which Ahab could only dream, and the looted sarcophagi of Pharaohs untold. What chance then a slender wisp of femininity such as yourself? I thought lunch on the *plage*, with supper at the casino and champagne on the terrace at midnight. I hope our waiter is a strong and capable youth. These train journeys enervate me so—to the point where buttering one's own teacake is quite beyond consideration. Ah, here is my ambulance and my nurse. It has been a pleasure knowing you, madame. Your fat buttocks and sweeping *mustachios* remind me of any number of naughty games involving multicolored handkerchiefs, jars of mustard, and photographs of the Duke of Windsor. A parting kiss. A sigh! Until next time, Monsieur—adieu!"

•

"Welcome to St Tropez, Mesdames et Messieurs. Enchanté!"

# Key Blanco #1

He was the only Chinaman who had ever held a commercial fishing license in Key Blanco and his silhouette, when he stood in the stern of his boat in either the early morning or the late evening, delicately steering through the mangrove channels that led to the freedom of the open sea, was reminiscent of an ink-brush painting, being of three slender strokes that made the curve of the boat and the straightness of the pole and the enigmatic Chinese character of the man himself, neither purely ink nor purely water, but very straight, and tall too—tall not just for a Chinaman, but for any man—and perfectly balanced against the movement of the sea. The name of the sea was the Straits of Florida and the name of the Chinaman was Song Qiang and he fished for yellowtail and snapper and filleted them himself on a trestle table he set up in the garden of the house he lived in on Flagler Street and then took them to the fish-house, insisting the scales were cleaned of fish blood and fish scales before he allowed his own to be weighed. The receipt for the weight of the fish he studied under the fluorescent light nearest the window and then smiled and folded it into the left-hand breast pocket of his faded-nearly-white blue denim shirt and then went to Bobbie's Clam Shack for a cigarette and a beer.

•

He had only managed to earn a commercial fishing license after three long years of trying, because the way they work it is this: They issue you a provisional license and then make it valid for ninety days and then set you a target for sales to the fish house that is impossible to meet. No fish not recorded by the fish-house is legal and no fish under twelve inches is legal and no fish is legal caught outside that window of ninety days. And if the target is not literally impossible, it is as near as humanly-possible impossible. Because if they cannot make commercial fishing a closed shop, they can at least sincerely damn-well try. One way to tilt the odds ever so slightly in your favor is to fillet the fish yourself before taking them to the fish-house—the rate is better pro rata for the work you save them, plus theoretically you can catch undersize fish and no-one will know. But fish are not just measured at the fish-house, they can be measured by coast guard inspectors at any time while your boat is on the water, and no true fisherman, no true Florida Keys fisherman anyhow, not from anywhere no matter how far, not even if far is as far as San Francisco or Shanghai, will deliberately keep an undersized fish. They may not be particularly honest men, they may cheat freely with cards and with landlords and with other men's wives, but they are old-fashioned in the way of all fishermen since the Phoenicians and have an atavistic respect for the laws and traditions of the sea—plus the fact that a legal inspector can suspend your license, fine you a maximum of $20,000 and impound your boat. Song Qiang had never filleted an undersized fish and therefore lived at peace, albeit an uneasy peace, as indeed did they all, with the gods of Monroe County and the old gods of Florida and the even older Gods of the sea.

•

During those three years he had often fished at night, firstly as a necessity during the intense ninety-day periods of trying to gain a license, but subsequently because he had formed an emotional attachment to the stars.

On one particular night Song Qiang had fallen asleep holding the rod despite being aware of a twelve or thirteen-foot shark circling his boat. The knowledge of the shark had begun because he had hooked a fish that he knew was a red snapper not less than two pounds in weight, knowing it to be a snapper not a yellowtail by the strength of its resistance to the hook. But just as he had drawn the fight out of it and was reeling it in there was a massive strike on his line, a strike that was as brief as it was violent, that would have torn the rod from his grip had not the shark that had taken his snapper almost simultaneously bitten through the wire tracer and left him in possession of an eight-foot rod with no more substance than a blade of grass.

That had been in the mid-afternoon, a mile or so beyond Pelican Key where there is a shelf that drops suddenly to about eighty feet and where, anchored on the edge of it, thirty minutes later, Song Qiang had seen the fin come up and slice the water and had said,

"Xian zai wo kan dao le ni, Sha yu, shi wo de yu de tou qie zhe."

and had surprised himself—not by speaking out loud, but by speaking in Chinese, a language he had spent the past several years unlearning and indeed had not spoken with any frequency or serious meaning since his time as a chef in San Francisco's Chinatown, since before his long journey by Greyhound that had culminated in far-away Key Blanco, finding himself at nearly midnight on a poorly-illuminated strip of dusty pavement and surrounded by Panama-hatted tourists and palmetto bugs. He repeated the sentence in English,

"Now I see you, Shark, who is a stealer of my fish."

and watched with satisfaction as the fin sank down below the level of the sea.

Four times between mid-afternoon and evening the shark had resurfaced, and no man who is alone in a seventeen-foot boat likes the company of a twelve or thirteen-foot shark, especially when night is falling and the boat seems to contract as the darkness expands. He said,

"Sha yu xian sheng, yi wang wu ji de hai yang, nin he wo de chuan dou you kong jian."

and then, afraid the fish might not understand,

"The ocean is big, Mister Shark, there is room enough for you and my boat."

and then strained his eyes to catch another glimpse of the slate-colored fin amongst the shifting slates that made the surface of the sea.

After that neither the end of the evening nor the beginning of the night was unusual other than that strikes on his line were reduced to one every ten or fifteen minutes and his catch by midnight hardly justified the effort of staying awake. He had reeled in then and lit a hurricane lamp and eaten the salami and blue cheese dressing sandwich and drunk half of the flask of sugar-stiffened black coffee that Mrs. Ramirez, his landlady, had made for him, and read the note (by the light of a match) that Mrs. Ramirez had written in china-graph pencil on the wax paper that wrapped his sandwich. It said,

**Thou rulest the raging of the sea: when the waves thereof arise, thou stillest them.** (Psalm 89)

and Song Qiang smiled and ate the sandwich and drank the coffee and imagined the shark carving its own messages through the ink-black strata of the sea ...

He awoke with a start and was immediately relieved to see that the rod was still in his hands and that the boat upon which he sat was still a boat and that the sea that surrounded the boat was only sea. He had been dreaming a strange dream in which he was sweeping the debris of peeled prawns from the pavement in front of a restaurant in Shanghai and large black American automobiles constantly drove past, jeering white-painted faces pressed against otherwise impenetrable glass. He reeled in a stripped hook and secured it in the guide nearest the reel and propped the rod against the fish box in the stern. He remembered there was still coffee in Mrs. Ramirez' flask and felt suddenly strong again, as though he had survived something or as though a task to be feared had been accomplished with neither loss nor pain.

The coffee was by now only barely-warm, but so heavily sweetened that it spread within him an almost rum-like sense of well-being. He leaned back against the wheelhouse and wondered at the beauty of liquefied sugar sliding over his tongue, and somehow knew that no shark would bother him again tonight. He said,

"Farewell, Mister Shark. Another time, maybe." He paused, he added, "my friend."

and leaned back his head and was contemplating the familiar beauty of the stars when

*sssssssssshwioo*

and knew that what he had never seen previously he had seen now—something more wonderful than contained in any of Mrs. Ramirez' psalms; a meteor plummeting from Heaven as though God had struck a match and let it fall. A shooting star.

•

He had docked at Key Blanco's Fishermen's Wharf shortly after sunrise and followed the usual routine of filleting his catch, delivering it to the fish house and then strolling down to Bobbie's Clam Shack for a beer and a cigarette. But he was uninvolved and taciturn, even by his normal standard of self-containment, and spent the rest of the morning at a table in the corner, barely acknowledging any greetings that came his way, wrapped in a cloak of solitude as impenetrable as any oilskin ever worn at sea.

•

So it was that Song Qiang went night fishing at least once, maybe even twice or three times a month, delicately steering his boat through the mangrove channels that led to the freedom not just of the open sea but also the open sky. If I spoke previously of emotional attachment that was because I hesitated to use the word love, and yet there can be no doubt that Song Qiang felt the same combination of anticipation and anxiety (as his boat picked up speed and headed out in the direction of Pelican Key) as a man in love with a woman might feel during the taxi ride to an all too infrequent rendezvous. But that is a poor analogy, for he loved the stars with a love that was simultaneously innocent and profound and felt in their presence a combination of wisdom and wonder such as might have been felt by holy men on mountain-tops in the land of his birth. He fished until midnight or thereabouts, poured out some coffee and allowed himself then the wonderful panorama of the stars. This is not to say that the nights were without drama—his friend the shark (or maybe the shark's brother) used his fin to slice a delicate fillet of salt water from next to the ribs of his boat and one time a loggerhead turtle, merely surfacing as a turtle might, neither with malice nor design, nearly tipped him sideways into the appalling vertigo of the open sea, but always Song Qiang returned home with at least an average catch and a sense of fulfillment, of spiritual equilibrium, of profound and abiding calm.

•

Mrs. Ramirez' husband had sailed from Havana to Key Blanco in a vessel that was little more than a jazzed-up banana crate and had lit off from Key Blanco to Miami in the company of an Americano nightclub singer who was little more than a jazzed-up waitress, leaving Mrs. Ramirez with nothing but an immigrant's work ethic and a fierce sense of injustice, both of which had been translated, six years later, into a small but popular Latino deli and a two-story house on Flagler Street, the upper floor of which she rented out, preferring to keep for herself the street-level convenience of strolling from her veranda and across the small width of garden to chat with passersby. It was the same small width of garden upon which her current tenant, Song Qiang, set up a trestle table in the afternoon three or four times a week to fillet the yellowtail and red snapper he had caught in the morning or two or three times a month in the morning to fillet the red snapper and yellowtail he had caught during the night. Notwithstanding the fact that Mrs. Ramirez was in love with Song Qiang and Song Qiang was not only not in love with Mrs. Ramirez but also naively unaware of the fact that there was even a love that he failed to reciprocate, theirs was a tenant / landlady relationship as nicely balanced as a boatman on a boat steering a passage through a mangrove channel, the coffee and sandwiches for his night fishing excursions graciously accepted as merely a token of appreciation for his unobtrusive presence upstairs and for the fact of his rent always being paid with punctilious regard for the day it was due.

•

Song Qiang reeled in a yellowtail, threw it into the fish box, and secured the hook in the guide closest to the reel. His shoulders ached pleasantly from a good night's fishing and he already knew that he would not have to take his boat out again for at least another four or five days. A small storm previously forecast to strike the Florida Keys at about three a.m. had been downgraded to a strong wind and repositioned thirty miles west, leaving him free to pour his coffee and unwrap his sandwich (Swiss cheese on rye) and enjoy his first proper scan of the night sky. There were several stars that he recognized instantly, greeting them as he might have greeted friends on first entering a crowded party,

"Ni hao, Xing Xiansheng, hen gao xing jian dao ni."

before turning his gaze in one beautiful and enormous sweep as though to gather into his soul the entire contents of the universe. Underneath his boat, his seventeen-foot boat, unseen, his friend, Sha yu, all twelve or thirteen foot of him,

"Sha yu xian sheng, yi wang wu ji de hai yang, nin he wo de chuan dou you kong jian."

circled in search of newly-hooked snapper or yellowtail, and in the well of Song Qiang's boat there was a folded square of wax paper upon which had been written, in china-graph pencil,

**He telleth the number of the stars; he calleth them all by their names. (Psalm 147)**

while on a veranda on Flagler Street Mrs. Ramirez looked up at the star-endazzled sky and said a prayer for a Chinaman on the rim of infinity, loved without knowing he was loved, anchored off Pelican Key.

# Key Blanco #2

There are no snakes on the Florida Keys, but one time on Assumption Key they found a totem nailed through the eye socket of a pirate's skull and around the shaft of it there was wound a length of tar-stained rope with a leather ferrule that gave it the impression of a head with a mouth and eyes. Always afterwards Assumption Key was obeah and it became a shame for a fisherman to anchor there, even in bad weather, and if any fisherman did so nobody knew about it, and if anybody thought they knew about it they either thought wrong or kept their thoughts to themselves.

•

Pablo Morales always crossed himself and said a Hail Mary when he landed his boat on Assumption Key. He felt through himself the judder of the keel against the course-grained sand of his landing place and simultaneously heard and felt the *slissssh* of the backwash of the wave that had pushed him forward onto the beach. He swung himself overboard and landed ankle-deep with hardened soles in the newly wave-wet coarse-grained sand. He gripped the gunwale of the prow of the boat and pulled it keel-complaining beyond the now-negated pull of the sea. There were dead coconut husks everywhere scattered. There were birds that screeched obscenities at him from within the foliage of the trees.

•

Pablo Morales was fourteen years old and lived with his mother and sister in Calle Cubano, which is not a single street but an area about the size of a baseball park, and which is situated in Key Blanco between Flagler Street and the sea. His sister was seventeen and very beautiful, very *elegant*, muy elegante, and his mother worked as a barista at Mrs. Ramirez' Latino deli on Thompson Street, and his father trod water five fathoms down beyond Pelican Key, the pearls that were his eyes forever gazing upwards at the rippling keels of fishing boats and the sleek torpedoes that were blacktip sharks and the ribbons of sunlight rippling in-between.

"If I have my father's boat, then I will be a fisherman like my father. Como mi padre."

"And do you want to die like your father? Como tu padre?"

"I will never die!"

But in truth Pablo had had a terrible fear of death ever since his father drowned three years before, a fear that was a constant presence, like the nimbi around the heads of saints and apostles in all the cheaply-printed and over-colored pictures that, in one variation or another, graced the walls of the majority of the houses in Calle Cubano. Dios te salve, Maria. Llena eras de gracia. El Senor es contigo. He fought against it because he was a man, a man with neither father nor brothers, a man with a mother and a sister, a mother who wore skin-tight lace-trimmed lycra visible hosiery and served cafe Americano in three different sizes, and a sister muy elegante also muy estupido who believed the shiny pages of the fashion magazines contained a passport to Miami the way boys who were pearl divers believed every oyster held a pearl. But the enemy that recognized a cease-fire during the daylight hours mounted a renewed offensive each night, and on many of those nights he woke up in his little attic room between the ceiling and the roof-beams and listened to the tapping of the palmetto bugs on the glass of the skylight and felt that he was looking up at tourists looking down at him through the inverted skylight of a glass-bottomed boat. And he would sit up off the mattress choking and drowning and then, when he was no longer gasping for breath, lay himself down again to sleep. Santa Maria, Madre de Dios, ahora y en la hora de nuestra muerte.

He owned a boat, this boy, which was not his father's boat—*that* was permanently anchored in Wreckers' Bight, paid for and maintained

"You're welcome, Pablito!"

by his father's old friend and companion in rum Captain Tomas Esperanza—but a boat nonetheless, a ten-foot skiff with a mast that he handled as well as any professional fisherman, for he had learned how to rig a sail and navigate a channel before he was ten years old. And on this vessel, strangely, he had no fear of death, it was as though the sea that had claimed his father had already taken too much and so declared an armistice, granting him the same freedom as was granted the fish and the birds. He was even allowed to make landfall on the otherwise uninhabited, the obeah, Assumption Key—although his visits there were rationed out, for he knew that Death did not like His benevolence taken for granted and that even the sign of the cross and the perfectly enunciated Hail Mary offered only limited protection in accordance with some unwritten and atavistic law.

Many days he hand-lined for red snapper or mahi-mahi and the fish that his mother and sister ate on those evenings took the wind out of their complaints as to why he had not been in school. Many days also he had no thought but to be alone with the sea. But on this day, he again brought his skiff onto the narrow coarse-grained beach of Assumption Key and, as always, the fear that was absent on the ocean returned as a quickening of his heartbeat and an involuntary shiver as might accord with the expression of having someone walk over your grave. Dios te salve, Maria. Llena eras de gracia. El Senor es contigo. Bendita tu eres entro todas las mujeres, y bendito es el fruto de tu vientre, Jesus. He crossed himself and jumped out of the boat. The familiarity of the wet coarse-grained sand between his toes and the necessary effort of pulling the skiff at least partly ashore settled the beating of his heart. Above him an ibis crashed out of its nest in the canopy trees and flapped away to the other side of the key.

Assumption Key was about five hundred yards wide and a break in the trees led to a small clearing in its center. Pablo never ceased to wonder how soon on such a small island one lost all sense of contact with the sea. In the clearing there was a mound and on the mound there was a simple wooden cross made of two slats from an orange crate and on the cross was written the name of his father and R.I.P. and a pair of dates.

This was not exactly the grave of Pablo's father, who drifted in search of eternal peace in the deep waters beyond Pelican Key, but the best approximation a twelve-year-old Pablo, telling no-one, not even Captain Tomas, was able to accomplish in the year subsequent to his father's death. Beneath the mound there was an orange crate minus two slats wrapped in a tarpaulin and containing a gaudily colored print of the Virgin Mary as Stella Maris, a fixed-spool reel, a fishing novel by Zane Gray, a denim shirt, a carpenter's pencil, a pair of sun-glasses, a wax candle, and a bottle of five-year-old Havana Club rum. There was also a Cuban cigar box containing medallions of St Francis of Paola and St Clare of Assisi, several coins, a box of matches and a Key West cigar.

Pablo kicked a coconut husk away from the mound. His father said, "Pablito."

"Father?"

"Come here, I have something for you."

Pablo's father was standing in the doorway of their home in Calle Cubano, still wearing his long-billed fishing cap, the jacket with brass buttons he thought made him look like a naval officer, muy Americano, only very slightly betraying the influence of the rum he had drunk with Tomas Esperanza, he said,

"Look."

and in the hand that he removed from his pocket there on the palm were two medallions on slender chains, the chains themselves dripping between his outstretched fingers like the wax of candles on an altarpiece. He put his hand on Pablo's shoulder and stood beside the boy in respectful silence and looked down at the grave with his name on the cross marking it. He said,

"Why have you buried the medallions I gave you?"

"I don't know, Father. It seemed correct."

"I am happy with everything you have done for me, but the medallions . . . You will need them for luck at sea and to protect from storms."

Pablo looked at where he wanted his father to be standing. He said,

"Then I shall buy two more and bring them here and show them to you and you will bless them and Santa Maria will bless them and they will protect me all the days I am at sea."

His father smiled. His hair was soaking wet and plastered to his head except for where it curled up at the temples and above his ears. Pablo was aware of how handsome his father was and how very few men would have had the features and the charisma to remain handsome even after they had been drowned. His father wore a white shirt that was torn in many places and transparent where it made contact with his arms and chest. A ribbon of seaweed hung from the waistband of his baggy cotton pants. His voice when he spoke came from very far away. He said,

"Adios, Pablito. Adios."

and a thin breeze blew through the branches of the canopy trees.

•

Pablo Morales heaved the boat away from the sand and into the water and hauled himself over the gunwale and pushed fully with the blade of an oar until he was at sea. The sea here in this part of the world, and most especially where it becomes shallow around the many keys that inhabit the Straits of Florida, is very beautifully clear, and even clouds of sandy mud stirred up by the feet of a fourteen-year-old Cuban boy, or by the keel of a fourteen-year-old Cuban boy's boat, thin out and settle rapidly, and then there is visibility very far down. You can see shoals of nearly larval barracuda zig-zagging as though to the pull of two alternating magnets, and then scattering like shrapnel as a sandbar shark smooths its way through the planes of the sea. You can see the debris of many long-lost pirate ships, and once in a very rare while the skulls of the pirates themselves. They sleep almost entirely hidden under the silt of the ocean bed, revealing nearly nothing except the occasional inkwell of an eye-socket or the eel-enabling corridor of an inner ear. If they possess knowledge of the treasure chests they looted from their masters, they speak none of it, neither now nor evermore. It is doubtful even if they have any memory at all.

Pablo Morales raised the sail on his ten-foot skiff. He said,

"Santa Maria, Madre de Dios, ruega por nosostros pecadores, ahora y en la hora de nuestra muerti."

And a man who had drowned three years before, whose eyes were pearls, who wore a sash of seaweed at his waist, reached up and brushed his bone-pared fingertips against the keel of his son, Pablito's boat.

"Amén."

# Key Blanco #3

A rnold Bickerson tied up at the jetty belonging to Bobbie's Clam Shack and took the revolver out of the chart box in the wheel house. He slid the revolver into the pocket of his leather aviator's jacket and struck a match to light his cigarette on the gunwale of his twenty-three-foot boat. The fog was so thick that it had a sense of carpentry about it, and the sea-facing windows of Bobbie's, despite being less than a stone's throw away, and despite it being only four o'clock in the afternoon, were vague amber lozenges in the overwhelming yellowish-gray of wet putty. Arnold Bickerson swung himself up onto the fog-slickened timbers of the old jetty. Their texture under the soles of his sneakers was that of the thinnest layer of fresh snow. The smoke from his cigarette was invisible in the thickness of the fog.

•

She owned the beauty parlor on East Front Street and was herself the most beautiful woman in the Florida Keys. She had what Ron Martello, owner of the bait and tackle store, called 'genuine beauty' which, when asked exactly what he meant by that, defined it as beauty not immediately obvious, but which, once recognized, was so profound as to make 'obvious' beauty so shallow that it was hardly beauty at all. Nine out of ten guys, Ron Martello continued, wouldn't look at her twice, but the tenth guy would stay in love with her for the rest of his life. I'm better with words than with math, but even I can figure that at least thirty guys must've looked at her, because Ron was a tenth and I was a tenth and so was Arnold Bickerson. Her name was Nikki Taylor and she owned the beauty parlor on East Front Street and she drove a station wagon with Alabama plates. Those plates were the only clue that had ever been offered as to the life she had lived before she arrived in Key Blanco. Like the Foreign Legion, it asked no questions about a new arrival's past.

•

"Some nights the fog's so thick could hide all of Hannibal's elephants in it. Soldiers 'n' all."

"What did ol' Senator say?"

"Said the fog's gettin' worse and won' get better."

"So why in hell he mention elephants then?"

The one they called The Senator, who was not a senator, nor indeed the possessor of any public office in the entire colorful history of his fifty-nine years, banged his glass on the counter like a justice bangs his gavel. He said,

"I referred, young man, to the celebrated Carthaginian general and the Second Punic War. But never mind, never mind. Landlord, I'll graciously accept another glass of your esteemed pachyderm piss before we move on to the serious business of Chivas Regal and tales of ancient heroics in days long past ... "

•

I earned a living best I could as a deckhand on shrimping boats and also wrote a weekly column on fishing for the *Key Blanco Citizen*. Deadline was Tuesday mornings 9 a.m. and at about 8.30 I'd roll the final sheet out of my vintage Royal portable, cycle over to the paper's premises on East Front Street, drink a cup of coffee and smoke a cigarette with the editor, and then walk my bicycle slowly past Nikki Taylor's beauty parlor in the hope I might see her when she was opening up. After that it was my habit to ride over to Bobbie's Clam Shack, Bobbie's being one of the four or five places that opened early and served beer and breakfast to the lonely, the unloved, the dispossessed, as well as night fisherman such as Song Qiang and would-be Faulkners or Hemingways such as myself. I have always loved bars in the early morning. There is an illicit thrill about ordering a beer when most of the world drinks coffee, and there is something special about the quality of the light through salt-smeared windows at that time, a particular shade of dusty yellow like the inside of a carpenter's shop. I'd drink a beer, maybe two, then bicycle on home.

•

The gun smelled of oil and metal and had the weight of an anchor in Bickerson's hand. He slid the gun into the pocket of his jacket and swung himself up onto the fog-slickened jetty. Coming as if from a foreign land he could hear the mournful sound of the foghorn on Prospect Key.

•

Ron Martello owned a fifteen-foot cabin cruiser just purely as a pleasure boat, and sometimes he'd take Nikki Taylor out of a Sunday, usually to Cayo Grande, which had a nice beach, a semi-circle or half-moon, depending on whether you were a mathematician or a poet, faced by a shallow sea and surrounded by palm trees. He'd take a picnic, some cans of beer, a bottle of Californian white wine, and come home letting Nikki steer the boat into Wreckers' Bight, both of them, in all fairness, tanned and salt-stained and smiling radiantly beneath their almost-matching Ray-Bans, two of the best-looking *nicest*-looking people you could wish to see. I loved Nikki Taylor with all my twenty-four-year-old heart, but was resigned to the fact that I was too young, too *callow*, too wrapped up in a writer's idea of romance, to ever achieve real success with a real woman of forty-five—never mind one as beautiful as that. Arnold Bickerson had the disadvantage of no such self-awareness. In short, he was jealous and none too bright—a savage combination visited by God only upon those who have grievously offended Him in a former life.

•

Arnold Bickerson stood on the jetty, feeling the cold and the damp of it through the soles of his sneakers, taking deep draws on the unfiltered Lucky Strike cigarette. The windows of Bobbie's Clam Shack glowed palely ahead of him, like the lights of an oncoming train when one has over-committed oneself to walk down the tunnel. He could no more turn around and lower himself back down into the boat and push off quietly from the jetty than, in a different scenario, he could've turned around and outrun the train. He smoked the cigarette down almost to his fingers and chucked the butt of it into an invisible sea. He touched the butt of the gun with his right hand. His jacket was damp from the dampness of the fog.

•

"It was on such a night as this that the Spanish vessel *Santa Anita* went down in the deep waters off Assumption Key. That was in the year of our Lord sixteen hundred and sixty-three. Twenty-four guns on each side of her and carrying in her hold a magnificent treasure intended as a gift to the governor of Florida from the King of Spain. Oh, what jewels, what ornaments, what finely-wrought artifacts of silver and gold must those steel-bound chests have contained! And all, all lost at the bottom of the sea . . . "

It was only four o'clock in the afternoon but the windows of Bobbie's Clam Shack were opaque with fog and the bar room itself had the atmosphere of a ship far out at sea. Very faintly in the distance they could hear the foghorn making its mournful mating call from Prospect Key. The Senator drained his glass of beer, filled it up again from the bottle beside it, examined the tip of his Dominican Republic cigar, and continued.

"Where was I? Ah, yes! The *Santa Anita* went down with all hands and all her treasure went down with her—or so they say. But legend has it that the night before she sank the captain anchored off Assumption Key and put down a small boat and rowed ashore with a chest of treasure and two carefully selected men. Even one chest, even a fraction of that extraordinary manifest, would have been riches beyond the dream of any seafaring man— and the captain, whose name was Rodriguez de la Castillo de Sevilla, was a seafaring man who dared to dream. He found a suitable spot and set those two unfortunate men to dig. I say unfortunate, because no sooner had the box been lowered into the hole than Captain Rodriguez drew a pair of pistols from his waist-sash and shot them both where they stood. They would go down in the log as deserters—a not unreasonable assumption that near to the Florida Keys. Little could they have known, when they were pressganged from some brothel in Cadiz, that they would end up in joint possession of a king's fortune. One is reminded of Chaucer, is one not? More specifically *The Pardoner's Tale*, but I digress, I digress. Where was I?"

Captain Jeffrey winked at Two-Buck Tony behind the bar. He said,

"In a brothel in Cadiz, Senator."

"I am Samson surrounded by Philistines. Landlord, take away hence from me this vile excuse for beer. A drink now prepare for me such as Achilles drank before the walls of Troy. I refer, of course, to a cup of Chivas Regal—*if* you please."

•

Nikki Taylor had her back to the sidewalk and was unlocking the door of her beauty parlor as I bicycled slowly past. I said,

"Good morning, Nikki."

and she looked over her shoulder and smiled and said,

"Good morning!" Then, "How are you?"

"I'm fine, thanks. Yourself?"

"Just fine."

If only she'd had her arms full of stuff, I could've offered to help her in with it all, but all she had was a key in one hand and a paper bag of some or other beauty products in the other. Her sunglasses were pushed back on top of her head. The collar of her plaid shirt was turned up. She looked utterly lovely. I wanted to say something important and memorable. I said,

"Well, so long. Have a nice day."

"You too."

I pressed down on the left pedal to gain traction and had just gotten restarted when she called out,

"Oh, by the way."

"Uh-huh?"

"I saw the piece you wrote in last week's *Citizen*. It was really good."

"You liked it?"

"I've shown it to all my customers." She smiled again. "Have a nice day."

I flew to Bobbie's, for how could the wheels of my bicycle even begin to touch the commonplace asphalt of a mere and vulgar road on such a glorious, such an extraordinarily perfect morning?

•

The door of Bobbie's Clam Shack swung inwards to reveal the hazy approximation of a figure in a swirling suffocating oblong of vivid yellow-gray. Tendrils of fog took advantage of the sudden aperture to snake their way at ankle height across the worn-down wooden floor. Tongues of fog like thirsty toads licked the inside of the framework of the door. The figure stepped over the threshold and became defined as Arnold Bickerson, now standing in bold relief against the fog billowing at his back. He came into the barroom beyond the arc of the door and closed it behind him with his right foot. There was an audible sigh from the fog that was trapped outside.

•

When Ron Martello first came to Key Blanco there'd been big talk about fishing charters out of Bimini and The Cayman Islands, and some pretty wild talk about running booze and cigars and even people out of Havana, but none of the big talk was his. It was the talk of the people he'd met those first few weeks, people who'd accepted his offer of a beer in The Blue Marlin and The Lighthouse Bar and Bobbie's Clam Shack, people who needed to weave a mystery around a stranger who was straightforward, open-handed, effortlessly likable, and bore a passing resemblance to Gary Cooper. By the time of his third visit, when it had become generally known (not without a certain disappointment) that he was selling up his tool and die business in Milwaukee and had put in an offer to buy the run-down bait and tackle store on Geddes Street, the limitations of his past (or lack of it) in respect of mystery-weaving were if anything an asset. There were and always have been plenty of shady not to say downright criminal characters in Key Blanco; an honest handsome man spending money honestly made was by way of a novelty, and a welcome novelty at that.

You don't notice something happening extremely slowly until it's done gone and happened, and then you look back and wonder where in the process the noticing should've begun. That's how it was with Ron Martello and Nikki Taylor. No-one knew a thing until that first time they came back from a picnic on Cayo Grande. But it was typical of his easy-going popularity, not forgetting the genuine respect in which he was held by all who had business dealings with him, that even those others who loved Nikki themselves, loved her from afar (and there were more than two), felt no grudge against Ron Martello, merely a gentle and whimsical sense of loss. A notable exception being Arnold Bickerson, who festered unchecked on single-handed three- or four-day deep-sea fishing trips and hated Ron Martello with all the passion of a sick and jealous hate.

•

Ron Martello was sitting by himself at one of the tables over by the far wall, reading last Sunday's *Miami Herald* and absent-mindedly drinking from a bottle of Miller Genuine Draft. He barely looked up when Arnold Bickerson entered the bar. Captain Jeffrey and The Senator were on stools by the counter, and there were maybe half a dozen other people scattered about. Myself, I was off on a shrimp boat, a three-day ride, but everything that happened I heard about later from Two-Buck Tony, who tended bar. He is what the literature professors call a reliable narrator. I assume so, anyway, because however many times the story got told it always stayed exactly the same.

Arnold Bickerson swung the door shut behind him with the back of his foot, walked into the center of Bobbie's Clam Shack, took the gun out his pocket, raised it to chest-height, and shot Ron Martello through the front page of *The Miami Herald*. Shot *at* Ron Martello might be more accurate. The bullet went through the paper, brushed the side of Ron Martello's head, and made a classic shatter-hole in the glass of an old maritime print—one of many that typically grace the walls of traditional waterfront bars. The noise, apparently, in that relatively small room was deafening, and surprised Arnold Bickerson as much as anybody else. Surprised him enough to stop him firing another shot, or should we say delayed him firing it long enough for Captain Jeffrey and one other guy to grab him and twist his arm back and force the gun out of his hand. It was a snub-nose Smith & Wesson .357 and it hit the floor like an anchor hitting rock.

Satisfied the gun was safe, Captain Jeffrey, a man with proven capability of landing an eight-hundred-pound marlin, stood square in front of Arnold Bickerson and dropped him with a straight right to the solar plexus. He didn't draw his arm back more than twelve inches and all the air went out of Bickerson like sticking a knife in a tire.

Of course, all this happened incredibly fast; it's just the telling makes it slow. No more than fifteen seconds had elapsed since the door swung open. And now everybody's attention turned to Ron Martello, who looked from Bickerson to the hole in the newspaper and then to Bickerson again, and then leaned around to look at the bullet hole in the picture-glass. Then he touched the right side of his head and winced. Whether the wince was with the pain of it or the nearness of it, Two-Buck Tony couldn't say. "The fog alters time, makes it move differently," he said. Then added,

"What everybody loved about it, loved about it afterwards, I mean, was it was old Key Blanco. Key Blanco before the tourists moved in and then the realtors. Bickerson's shot was like Emerson's—not heard around the world, exactly, but pretty loud in the Florida Keys."

•

It was a bad trip, for a shrimping vessel. Nobody liked each other, the catch was low, and the bycatch included an otherwise healthy turtle for each of the three days we were out. One night I leaned on the starboard rail and drank rum from a flask in my 'skins pocket and smoked a cigarette and looked out at the moonlight glittering over the Gulf Stream. Almost needless to say, I thought about Nikki Taylor. I thought about Nikki and me somewhere romantic, like Bimini. I thought about her wearing a wet swimsuit on a sun-lounger and drinking a pina colada. When I chucked the cigarette overboard it flared briefly and then disappeared.

•

The Senator poured a splash of water into his glass from a jug on the counter. He said,

"Ah, Chivas Regal. Watered by Niobe's tears."

and Captain Jeffrey took a cigarette out of the pack that was laying on the bar and struck a match on the underside of his stool. Two-Buck Tony wiped the counter with a dishcloth and Arnold Bickerson, older, sorer and, one hoped, at least a little wiser, sat over at one of the tables drinking the bottle of Budweiser Ron Martello had bought for him. Ron Martello himself had had a quick shot of tequila on the house and then headed off to tell Nikki Taylor what had happened for real before she heard it for gossip. I myself, as I have said, was out on a shrimping boat, nearer Cuba than where all the action was, working my way on a miserable trip home.

And through it all the fog was so thick you could've cut it with one of Song Qiang's filleting knives.

# The Fractured Wor[l]ds of Willem Kleist

"**M**ostly what made him matter was, he didn't give a damn. He was the only one of us who didn't. I mean, who *really* didn't. Yes, *yes*, we all played the game, we were cool, a poem, a story, a painting, whatever, was no more important than a Gauloises cigarette, a book of matches, the way you slouched on a street-corner with your hands in your pockets, an obscene word painted with your girlfriend's lipstick on the bathroom mirror of a hotel in Pigalle, a page torn out of a magazine and stuck on a canvas with your own spit. But don't believe we ever *really* thought like that. Shit, man, no! I guarded, we *all* guarded, our manuscripts, our cahiers, our typescripts just totally ready for Gallimard, for the collected works, for the Academie Francaise. To the best of my knowledge, there's only ever been two writers whole of history showed complete indifference their own work. The other was Rimbaud."

•

In the theatre of war
only the tenderest will survive.
Snowflakes. And ladies
with fashionably slender cigarettes.
Paint brushes
in empty olive jars
and sudden yellow hats
in silent stairwells
hiding
from the rain.

•

"Well, we've pretty much discussed your poetry, Mister Kleist. Fine poetry it is too. But here's a kind of a light-hearted wrap question. Just to finish off. Who do you rate the greatest pound-for-pound writer of all time? And what's your opinion of Sugar Ray?"

A pause while Kleist taps the ash off his cigarette.

A longer pause.

"James Joyce. Maybe Jack Dempsey. Gene Tunney. The only person I ever met be scared to go fifteen rounds with is Anais Nin. Also, Isadora Duncan. Whom I met only one time, briefly. You mean Sugar Ray Robinson?

Saw him on TV against La Motta. Like reading Kafka through broken spectacles. Writers go fifteen rounds every day against a typewriter and a stack of paper. Fuck writers. Fuck boxers. Fuck interviews. That's all."

•

Roosevelt Elected for Third Term!
Basil Rathbone
Boris Karloff
Bela Lugosi
in *Son of Frankenstein*

•

"The most perfect work of art I ever saw was Natalia Goncharova's brassiere hanging from a hotel door-knob, reflected in the bathroom mirror while Natasha herself was taking a shower. It would have been impossible to replicate the impression it made on me in any sonnet or cinematograph. The circumstances, moreover, were somewhat unusual. I observed the scene closely with a telescope from the basket of a hot air balloon during an (unsuccessful) attempt to circumnavigate Orson Welles."

•

Even when Birgitte
sucks my cock
I am obsessed by the absinthe
of a blue giraffe.

•

"William Klein? Yeah, sure, of course. Paris nineteen twenty-five. Or maybe it was San Francisco? Nineteen sixty-eight? Sorry, son, my hearing's not—Oh, *Kleist*. William *Kleist*. Hell, no, never heard of him. Charles Bukowski, heard of him. Richard Brautigan. Mowed his lawn once. Used to be a gardener. Knees not what they used to be. Nobody listens any more. Nobody speaks up. Whole world going deaf. Mind you don't spill that beer, son. Linoleum's like grease on a bear's ass get it wet. I should know. Owned a bear once. Yosemite, nineteen thirty-seven. Or maybe Yellowstone? Nineteen fifty-three? Sorry, what was that, Willem who? Never mind, son. Jus' you mind that there linoleum. Slicker'n a penguin's flipper. Slicker'n rain."

*

The ceiling
of the Café Kafka
is the color
of the underneath
of an antique postage stamp.
The bears rattle their chains
on the cobblestones
of the streets
of the Black Light Theatre.
The cigarettes
of the tram drivers
glitter in the darkness
like knives.

*

"All this stuff about the nineteen-twenties is so ridiculous. We were just kids then. With new toys. Not geniuses at all. Bunuel with his movie camera. Man Ray re-inventing the nude. Jesus, I only wrote poetry because I was too shy to paint myself blue and stand on a dead chimpanzee in the Bois de Boulogne."

"And yet it would appear that despite, maybe even *because* of, your reluctance to take your own work seriously, you were greatly admired by most of your contemporaries. I'm thinking specifically of Jean Cocteau, when he said, Willem Kleist is the metronome in a discordant age."

"Did it occur to you that might've been an insult?"

"It's pretty generally assumed to be a compliment. And, after all, you and Cocteau were good friends."

"Baloney. Cocteau was nobody's good friend. Now, if you'll excuse me, I need to go to the bathroom."

*

There is no silence
like the silence
of a penguin's orgasm
in a wide-brimmed straw hat
during a matinee performance
of *Pelleas et Melisande.*

*

Willem Kleist (b. Prague 1899; d. New York 1983) was an expressionist /
surrealist film-maker in the nineteen-twenties and then a poet whose
work was designed to be popular with the mannequins in the windows
of fashionable boutiques [as well as with mothers who stick pins in their
children to inflict pain on their dolls].

*

O fabulous entreaties of ruined cities!
O sinister bereavements of broken alleyways!
The beggars who crawl through the shattered remains of Byzantium
are my *escargots* in garlic butter.
Black leather goggles are my Champs Elysees and my twisted penis
removes and repenetrates the cork in any number of [un]willing maidens.
And in the evenings
when the lamps are lit
brutal pastiche plays chess with the dismembered relics of Troy
& Carthage,
Lesbos & Greece.

*

"I'd like now, if I may, to turn our attention to a film you made in nineteen
twenty-four, quite near the beginning of your career. I think you—and
probably most of our viewers—know the film I'm referring to. It's called
*Calypso / Odysseus*."

"Sounds vaguely familiar."

"Well, let me jog your memory. In a recent poll of critics in *Sight and
Sound* magazine it was voted one of the three best experimental films of the
nineteen-twenties, only slightly behind *The Cabinet of Dr. Caligari* and *Un
Chien Andalou*. I'm sure you recall it now."

"What in fuck magazine?"

"*Sight and Sound*."

Willem Kleist takes a cigarette out of a cigarette case. Snaps the
cigarette case shut. Slips it back into his inside breast pocket. Strikes a
match. Lights the cigarette. Leans back to exhale a plume of smoke.

"I do barely recall that the movie was silent and nobody bothered to see
it. I recall also that I cast a new German actress in the part of Calypso. I can't
remember her name."

"Annie Vos."

"If you say so. I used to forget every movie I made as soon as I made it. This one was no exception."

•

The matador's dead
on a blood-stained Sahara.
A whore wearing blue spectacles.
A cop like an aubergine.
An aubergine holding a parasol.
A parasol holding a lady on a street in Paris illuminated by the sun reflected in the wing-mirror of an Indian motorcycle somewhere between a town in Texas and Albuquerque, New Mexico.
Saint Sebastian shot dead with cactus needles.
Read all about it! Catholic ikon sucks Jesus' cock!
Drops down decap/itated crimson rain.
Dead matadors ten.

•

"It was at one of those Manhattan cocktail-parties for Leonard Bernstein. This old woman, eighty-seven eighty-eight years old, wearing incredibly red lipstick, started asking me about typewriters. I told her I owned five, but that my favorite was a 1928 Royal with perfectly round silver-rimmed ivory keys. She said, 'Do the keys have letters on them?' She was holding an empty martini glass still containing the olive. My immediate impression was of senile dementia, exacerbated by alcohol. But then I got this beautiful sense of joy. A typewriter with blank keys! What a great surrealist image! I immediately 'phoned Sigmund Freud. Something I would have been much too shy to do were he still alive."

•

Six naked whores
in a Chinese elevator
are as impossible
as a purple typewriter
on a butterfly's wing.

•

"The most perfect work of art I ever saw was a car smash in Berlin. Blood everywhere. Black metal. Broken glass. The white face of some fat bastard's wife framed in a twisted window. Red paint in her fish-tank empty eyes. Her damaged breasts spilling out of her sheer silver gasoline-ignited opera dress. *Flapper-flapper-flapper-flapper-flapper.* The way a movie is when the spool runs out. *Flapper-flapper. Flap-flap.* Nice teeth. Decent bone structure. A split bitch screaming. Machete watermelon. Everybody melting. Behind the flames."

●

Monsieur Buerre-Couteau
dived through the tropical blue of Balenciaga
indifferent to the seagulls and shop-girls and Boris Karloff impersonators,
oblivious to the derision
of his wife and their three children and their local coal merchant (M. Brique-Noir).
Oblivious to everything (in fact).
Oblivious even to the excessive slurping noise of M. Le Mosquite sucking the blood out of the blue-tinged oxygen-starved suspender-sanctified thigh of a No. 83 London bus conductress in a Shanghai noodle shack.
Oblivious.
Ob. Livious.
Ob.

●

"Thank you, Mister Klein, it's been a pleasure."
  "I wish I could say the same."

# Varii Graffiti

H e leaned back against a wall beside the River Neva, one leg bent at the knee, the sole of his sneaker flat against the white stone, the sleeves of his sweater rolled up to his elbows, his French beret set at a jaunty angle, a cigarette dangling from the corner of his mouth,

## TOLSTOI Y TROTSKY ESTAN MUERTOS!

painted in letters six feet high on the otherwise pristine marble wall.

•

They met in cafes and bars and bistros in cities as diverse as Paris and Krakow and New York. They wore clothes that were only appropriate for the movie in which they wished themselves to be. I was a sickly child, a cripple who'd contracted polio at the same age Mozart was when he wrote his Symphony No. 5 in B-flat, a kid who wore tinted spectacles to shield himself from the anger of the sun. Precocious, abandoned, allergic to all but the shelves of books that towered from floor to ceiling in my uncle's atelier, having no friends but the sparrows I fed with breadcrumbs on the slender balcony that looked down on an indifferent street, I lived and loved vicariously, insulated from life the better to experience it. My uncle, blind and paralyzed, stared with passionate intent at a vast and interior landscape populated with pageants of fake-medieval pre-Raphaelite joy, mumbling only when, with an enormous effort for my crippled nine-year-old frame, I tilted him from one half of his backside to the other—not to improve his internal, entirely subjective view, but to better spread the wear-and-tear on the worm-eaten wooden supports of the antique sofa on which he barely lived and so persistently dreamed. If *he* dreamed of The Blessed Damozel, *I* dreamed of all those meetings in the cafes and the bars and the bistros, tilting glasses of Sauvignon Blanc or Zywiec Beer or Manhattan cocktails, leaving smears of paint on otherwise pristinely polished counters, wearing long coats the texture of carbon-paper, sporting silk scarves casually draped around unshaven necks, acknowledging the covert smiles of waitresses that led to inevitable kisses blown through the smoke-plumed air. These were the heroes of my anarchic invention and I looked forward to when they were published as a series of cigarette cards, even buying a container of Gloy glue in anticipation of owning the album in which they, like flies in amber—no, like flies on flypaper—would be permanently stuck . . .

•

He stepped back from one of the Ionic columns of the Temple of Zeus and used the handle of his paintbrush to tilt back the brim of his hat. A globule of red paint hesitated on the end of a bristle then landed *splat!* exactly between his rope-soled espadrilles. He took a swig from the bottle of Metaxa that he had been holding in his other hand and smiled the beautiful smile of a matinee-idol spider admiring a Brigit Bardot kind of fly. In the meantime

## I KNOW HOW MEN IN EXILE FEED ON DREAMS

had been written around the column like a tattoo on a sailor's arm.

•

Their names were unknown to all but themselves. If ever they had faces, those faces were no more than the masks in Greek plays. I hoisted myself from desk to chair to mantlepiece, cursing my spindly, useless legs, flinging myself like a sticky-fingered frog against the bookcase that contained Drama from A to B. Did I honestly think that I could write the unwritable by reference to those who, even in my precocity, wrote in languages, in idioms, that I was too ignorant, too unlearned, to understand? I ran my poor hands down the cloth-bound spines and then laid my withered cheek against the gilded lettering of *Prometheus Bound* and then *Mother Courage and Her Children*, reading Drama from Aeschylus to Brecht as though it were braille. Down on the street the siren of a fire engine provided its own soundtrack to another night of wildly illustrated dreams.

•

They learned to fly vintage aeroplanes and, with cannisters attached to their wings, painted revolutionary slogans across the canvas of the sky. They found a woman sleeping outside a temple of Lakshmi in Karnataka and inscribed a line from *The Upanishads* on her eyelids. They lined up for a photograph in the studio of a celebrated London-based fashion photographer, each of them wearing children's party masks, a cat, a dog, an elephant, a bear. Behind them, painted on an otherwise white backdrop,

## NIETZSCHE DIED SO THAT CHRIST MIGHT LIVE

And thus they appeared as lavish spreads in the pages of British and French and American *Vogue*.

•

I love windows that look out over rooftops, I love the angles and awkward silences, the mountains and valleys made out of brick and slate, the lush forests of lichen and the steppes of lead flashing, the chimney pots like sullen factories, blossoming out smoke and silhouetted against a starlit sky. How many hours, how many *hundreds* of hours, did I spend looking out of my uncle's attic skylight, twisting my already twisted body to encompass the entire panorama of an unknown city, a city of hats and hat brims with never a knowledge of the faces just underneath? I, who rocked myself to sleep in the crib of my agonized fantasies, knew nothing but delighted wakefulness when I prized open the ancient casement and soared over the rooftops of the city, swooping past yellow-lit windows, glancing down through skylights much as my own, skylights that looked down on the lonely, the burningly passionate, the defiantly enabled, running the tips of my fingers along soot-begrimed eaves and using those same soot-blackened fingertips to write

## VARII GRAFITTI TI AMO

across the cracked and blue-veined tiles that made the wall above my uncle's equally ugly, equally blackened galley-kitchen stove.

•

And if they did not have names, that was not for the lack of names I gave them. I remember when I was six maybe seven years old, being dragged through an old street by an even older nursemaid, an old street in the old quarter of the city where all the angles were wrong and the windows were yellow squares painted on gloomy wood and brick facades. It was a trip we made every Saturday, a visit to the Jewish Cemetery in the oldest part of the old quarter where her grandfather was buried, the victim of some purge or pogrom instigated by some century-old Kaiser or Tsar. The tombstones echoed the strange angles of the buildings that surrounded the small but crowded plot, moldering slabs of decomposing stone, many with the texture of pumice and hideously disfigured with the evil excrescence of lichen and moss. What names they might have been engraved with had mostly been lost, only random letters, some in English, others in Hebrew or Cyrillic, allowing the living to separate the dead. Oh, how I hated those weekly excursions, only made possible because the nursemaid, Mariska, answered to nobody, my parents being dead themselves (though buried far away elsewhere) and my uncle already nine-tenths living / dying in a world of his own devising. Even on the brightest summer day the ancient Jewish Cemetery was as gray as December and nearly as cold. Immediately I was pulled, whimpering, through the rusty iron gate I was conscious of my bare legs and the thinness of the material of my jaunty and hopelessly inappropriate sailor-suit. I stumbled over horizontal headstones, scraping my unprotected shins and smearing my pristine white knickerbockers against the collapsed and rotting memorials of the forgotten dead. I experienced that same sense of injustice and anxiety that made my weekday classmates in the Lycee simultaneously desperate to go to the bathroom and too fearful to ask to be excused. I said,

"Mariska, why must we go here?"

and was always answered with a muttered oath and a renewed pressure on my already twisted arm.

An irony at once beautiful and grim is that after the polio that cut my legs from under me and made all such excursions impossible, I was completely unable to remember anything whatsoever about the actual location or appearance of her grandfather's much-visited grave. The streets of the ghetto, the houses, the windows, the view of the madly random tombstones through the rotting filigree of the gate—these I could no more forget than the iron cages that were clamped around my miserable useless legs. But the grave itself . . . I said,

"Where is Mariska?"

and the nurse glanced at the doctor and the doctor nodded and the nurse said,

"Why, Yuri? Do you miss her?"

"No."

"Are you sure?"

"Very sure. Will my uncle be sad if I can't walk anymore?"

"Why do you say that, Yuri? Do you think he mightn't be?"

"I don't know."

There was a gauzy white curtain in front of the open window that billowed slightly inwards with the breeze. I liked that curtain very much and wanted to touch it, but my bed was too far away. I said,

"Tolstoi y Trotsky estan Muertos!"

and there were voices from outside that sounded like the voices of people in wheelchairs shouting out greetings to other people in wheelchairs. Or maybe cheerful people with the cushioned handles of crutches under their arms, crutches that made them swing like Sunday morning church bells. I said,

"I would be grateful for a glass of water. If it's not too much trouble."

and turned my face to the window. The sky through the breeze-blown gauze of the curtain seemed very far away.

•

# VARII GRAFITTI E IL NOSTRO NOME!

•

"Mariska," I said, "please let me go."

We had taken a slightly different route to the grave of Mariska's grandfather—the path that led directly, or at least as directly as the paths in the old Jewish Cemetery could possibly lead, was blocked by an elderly lady pushing an ancient gentleman in a chair with two sets of enormous and tiny wheels. The gentleman was wrapped in several blankets and wore spectacles with tinted blue lenses and silver rims. I said,

"Mariska, *please.*"

and broke away from her grip on my wrist and went to stand in front of a tombstone upon which the original chiseling had been worn almost entirely away but across the face of which had been quite recently painted

## FYODOR ISAAC DOSTOYEVSKY

although the lichen underneath the paint had, like some kind of allergic rash, already started to show through.

•

In all those subsequent nights of gazing over moonlit rooftops, in all those silent days surrounded by the walls of my uncle's books, I created a world for myself that needed heroes, heroes of my *own* invention, not the heroes of the library, of Mallory or Byron or Dumas, nor the heroes of boys, my contemporaries, from whose society I was cruelly excluded, for example Biggles the aviator, Batman the Caped Crusader, Captain Kirk of the USS Enterprise. On what occasion did I reach out my arm and run my extended finger down the face of the moon and realize that I could paint my frustrated desire on all the surfaces of the world?

## EROI CLANDESTINI DI PAZZO GRAFITTI!

I propelled myself with awkward jerks around a table piled high with literary bric-a-brac and crashed open the balcony doors. There were three sparrows on the railing, none of which flew off but, on the contrary, looked at me with their quick bright eyes in anticipation of food. There had been a shower of rain through the sunshine and piles of oranges and peppers and tomatoes gleamed in the wooden boxes that extended from underneath the faded red and blue awning of an épicerie down on the opposite side of the street. Strolling along the pavement a man carrying a cannister of spray-paint looked up at me, made eye contact, gave me a beautiful smile and raised the cannister in a gesture between a salute and a wave. It was like physical contact, an embrace. I had never seen such a beautiful smile before.

•

I called him Jonquil Clearwater and he was the first to be named.

## VIVA LA REVOLUCION!
## VIVA LA FRUTA Y LAS VERDURAS!

And soon I had a whole *Dramatis Personae*, as fine a crew as ever sailed in the *Argo* or stood before the walls of Troy.

•

They were international miscreants, unafraid to paint the lids of people's eyes. They were charismatic and enigmatic, intellectual and playful, and if ever they used a stick it was intended as a prop, a means to a certain elegant swagger, rather than as a tool to give a cripple traction across a lonely, book-lined room. In addition to Jonquil Clearwater, possessor of the world's most beautiful smile, there was Boris Velasquez, who painted the names of writers and revolutionaries on St. Petersburg's marble walls, and Lazarus Pope,

"Excuse me, young man, *whom* did you say?"

"Lazarus Pope, madam."

"A *most* unlikely name."

who decorated with extraordinary swirls of primary color the tombstones and headstones and memorial monuments of the world's most illustrious dead. From an island in the Aegean, an island so small that its name has never been recorded in either atlas or nautical chart, came Penny Arcadia, the Aerosol Queen, and out of the tenements of Brooklyn, littered with the debris of unfulfilled hopes and broken dreams, appeared Jill Jalapeno, her sister in crime, whose specialty was signing her name across the plate-glass windows of shady boutiques selling sky-high thigh-high rubber and latex fetish gear, herself wearing only a white plastic trench coat and a pair of nine-inch stiletto heels—

# JALAPENO SUX CUM XXX

Jack Dauncey danced across the rooftops of Paris, weaving sparklers to write poems on the midnight sky, and Lorenzo Sloop, wearing a thick white polo-neck sweater and a blue jacket with brass buttons, sailed around the world on fishing trawlers and cargo vessels and rich men's yachts, painting quotations from Conrad and Captain Nemo on the walls of waterfront brothels from San Francisco to Shanghai. Meanwhile, lurking in the shadows, wearing a mask that one moment made him resemble a gentleman cat-burglar, the next a character from the Comedia del Arte, was Sebastian Scaramouche—

"You, sir, are nothing but a sick young hoodlum!"

"Yes, ma'am, I have that reputation."

who had the ability to blend into the fog or dissolve in a shower of rain.

They were mine. They belonged to the world, but more significantly they belonged to me. I stumbled out onto my uncle's balcony and shouted out their names, creating them as aboriginal people once created all the things of the earth. The tears streamed down my cheeks and I felt I must literally glow with the force of my own emotion. Then the names that I had shouted I whispered, and down on the street Jonquil Clearwater and Boris Velasquez, Penny Arcadia and Jill Jalapeno, Lazarus Pope and Jack Dauncey and Lorenzo Sloop, one by one proceeded along the street, each glancing upwards to give me a mock-severe smile and a military-style salute . . .

Then, after four or five minutes had elapsed, slipping in and out of the shadows, wearing a cape that swirled around his ankles and a Venetian carnival mask, I glimpsed Sebastian Scaramouche, who acknowledged my presence in what must've seemed like the balcony of a theatre with a beautifully elaborate bow.

•

In the winter of that year it snowed heavily and the rooftops that I loved so much were more beautiful still. I discovered a taste for my uncle's plum brandy, several bottles of which I'd discovered by accident in an old armoire and a small glass of which was sufficient both to warm me and produce the mildest of intoxications, allowing my soul to leave my body for several minutes at a time, giving me the extraordinary capability of balancing on chimney pots with an acrobat's legs and seeing the city spread out beneath me like a Russian fairy tale. One night I drained off another glass, two glasses, three, and unbuttoned my trousers and urinated over a canvas of snow-layered slate, a quotation from Rimbaud

## J'AI SEUL LA CLEF DE CETTE PARADE SAUVAGE

a purple pastiche of a sudden and liberated joy! Purple and yellow, like an over-ripe plum.

•

When my uncle finally died two women arrived to take charge of the corpse. They were neighbors, one from the next-door apartment who would sometimes be hanging out washing at the same time as I was feeding the sparrows, the other from the same building as ours, but the floor lower down. They were both in their fifties and both quite thin, but one of them was tall and one of them was short. They wore severe black, of course, and looked at me with a mixture of pity and contempt. I was happy to sit quietly in the shape of a question-mark and read one of my uncle's books. They laid his body out in the bedroom, leaving the door open so I could see. They argued about everything, but in exaggeratedly low voices, the way people talk in church. They argued about whether he should be buried with his watch-chain, and what shoes he should wear, and whether to put pennies on his eyes. Then they argued about whether the pennies should be simply placed over the eyes or else screwed into the sockets like a pair of monocles. The taller one said,

"Yuri."

"Yes, ma'am."

"Come and look at your uncle before they take him away."

I levered myself off the chair in which I had been reading Montaigne's *Essays* and lurched into the bedroom. The pennies they had chosen were new and shiny and to me he looked more alive than he had for at least the past three years. It was a shame they were burying him when he looked so well. They'd even added a touch of rouge to his cheeks. I said,

"Goodbye, Uncle."

and then, in a genuine whisper that the two women, both of whom, anyway, had discovered the plum brandy, would be unable to hear,

"Don't worry about a tombstone, like Mariska. I've made some wonderful new friends, and if I ask them nicely, they'll paint your name all over the world. On buildings and churches and rooftops and—oh, even on the sky if you want them to."

I hesitated. I remembered he'd probably never even noticed the invention of the aeroplane. I said,

"Or on the sides of trams, if the sky seems a bit too ambitious."

I went back into the drawing room. The two ladies had finished very nearly a whole bottle of the plum brandy and were arguing about whether it had been made with French plums or English plums. The shorter one said,

"Well, Yuri, you've got to take care of yourself now."

She said it like she knew I wouldn't be able to. I said,

"That's right,"

and went out onto the balcony. It was a lovely spring morning, a little misty and still quite chilly, and down on the street the owner of the épicerie was putting the finishing touches to his display. He disappeared inside the shop, then reappeared with a box of mixed peppers, red and yellow and orange and green. The box neatly fitted into a gap on the slatted wooden framework that extended onto the pavement. He admired his handiwork and then, for no reason I could discern, half turned and looked up over his shoulder at exactly where I was standing. He smiled a beautiful smile and raised his hand in something between a wave and a salute. Gripping the railing of the balcony firmly with my left hand I returned his greeting with my right. I wanted to shout something, but my chest was too weak. But at least I was able to smile and he smiled again and repeated the gesture. Then he disappeared back underneath his awning. I leaned on the railing with my elbows and used the backs of my hands to wipe the tears from my eyes. I gulped for breath. I had never known such overwhelming happiness before.

# The Fishermen of Dragon-Tooth Beach

We anchored the rowboat and waded the last hundred yards ashore. The water was barely above our ankles, but we had to pick our way through a miniature forest of mangrove shoots five ten fifteen inches high, laid out like a tank trap between us and a narrow wedge of sand.

High on the beach four fishermen were stowing their gear. Their boat was drawn up almost to the tree line. There was a narrow road between the jungle and the bay. A fifth man came out of the jungle and joined them. They stopped what they were doing to watch us negotiate a path through the mangrove cones.

The girl slipped in the thick gray mud and I reached out instinctively to steady her. Feeling my hand on her bare shoulder she jerked away, almost slipping again. We continued forward in silence. There were no birds and the sea behind us was dead calm. The only sound was that of our feet squelching and glooping in the mud. The girl's legs were plastered blue-gray to the hem of her short sarong. The girl made the beach and I followed her.

It felt strange suddenly to be walking on sand.

We walked together up the sharp incline of the beach. The girl waved and one of the fishermen waved back. They had been rolling nets into tight cylindrical bales. One of these bales was already stowed in the back of a two-wheeled cart. The cart could be pulled by a donkey or pushed by a man. The others were folded, waiting to be rolled. The men were either bare-chested or had on unbuttoned sun-bleached shirts. They all wore torn mud-stained shorts. To their right, our left, was a raised pallet of bamboo poles, shaded by a palm leaf awning. A boy sat there, swinging his legs and smoking a cigarette. I hadn't noticed him until then, but he smiled at the girl.

Now that we were up close I could see that all the men were smiling. We exchanged cheerful hallos! and the man who had waved shook our hands. He looked sixty but was probably ten years less. His forehead bore the welts and discolorations of many hours and many storms at sea. At his hip there was a sheathed machete with a wooden haft. He nodded and grinned and said something to the others. They all laughed and came over and shook our hands. They were all very impressed with the girl. I don't know if they had ever seen a very beautiful, very tall blonde woman before.

My god, I thought, they are all so happy. Here they are, stowing their gear for the thousandth time and so obviously enjoying themselves. And would be even if we hadn't come along. A thin breeze tugged at my polo shirt and rustled the banana leaves.

The girl was talking to one of the other fishermen. He had two large suckerfish scars on his chest that put me in mind of the marks left by limpets on a rock. He was very handsome and had the dispassionate eyes of a man more used to looking at large expanses of sea. While he and the girl were talking the older man went and fetched two green coconuts from a small pile by the roadside. He came back beside us and grinned. When he unsheathed the machete, I saw that it was straight-ended, like a cutlass, and almost black from salt air and much use. Having prepared the first coconut for drinking, he gave it to me and I automatically passed it to the girl. She turned briefly and shook her head. He used the machete again, a sequence of swift economical hacks, and offered the second coconut to the girl. She smiled very brightly and then, looking down at this strange object in her hands, laughed, and all the fishermen laughed too, the cigarettes clamped between their teeth vibrating like tuning forks.

I lit a cigarette of my own and looked back at where we had walked ashore. The watery mud was a flat gunmetal gray, cleated with those obscenely exposed mangrove shoots. In our boat, completely beached now that the tide had receded several yards further, I could quite distinctly see a man and a girl. The man said something and the girl threw back her head and laughed. Her hair flashed in the shallow-angled late-afternoon sunlight. Then she leaned forward and put her arms around the man. I turned away quickly, and when I looked back they were no longer there.

The girl, this girl, had put aside her coconut and was smoking one of the fishermen's cigarettes.

# toreador pants and a white cotton shirt

H arry's 1958 Thunderbird turned off the road and onto the beach. All four doors swung open and we each of us got out. It was six in the morning and the beach was deserted. The sea was purple and the sky was orange and the horizon a thin line of green. Harry took a handgun out of the glove compartment and started shooting at an empty Budweiser bottle that Billy-Ray had thrown out into the sea. Billy Ray took another bottle out of the crate in the trunk and went and stood over on Harry's left, watching the spurts of water the bullets kicked up, tilting the beer in a long smooth swallow while Harry reloaded out of a box on the driver's seat. Eight-Ball Eddie had wandered off up the shoreline some ways and was holding a bottle of Four Roses and skimming coins across the surface of the sea. I felt a little cold and kind of sat / kind of leaned back against the hood of the Thunderbird, gripping my own bottle of Bud between my knees while I lit a cigarette. I'd had the idea of a story taking better and better shape in my mind during the whole time we were in The Blue Parrot. It had survived the noise of the jukebox and a whole load of tequila shots and eight or nine games of pool and it would be sad to lose it now, now that we were out at the beach. I inhaled and exhaled and imagined I was in my college room and sitting in front of my Remington portable and typing it down. *It had been raining for nine days. The color had long ago bleached out of the world and the cupolas and the domes and the rooftops were pewter-gray.* Imagining typing a story was a good way not to lose it. I visualized the keys hammering a sheet of paper and mentally slammed the carriage shift each time Harry shot a bullet into the sea.

•

It had been raining for nine days. The color had long ago bleached out of the world and the cupolas and the domes and the rooftops were pewter-gray. Even the sky was saturated, and rippled in the breeze like a photograph in a developing tray. She said,

"Do you remember Thailand? It rained so hard the street became a river. A boy caught a fish with a fishing rod from the balcony opposite our apartment."

"I remember."

"And that time in Key Blanco? People rowed boats down Perry Street. We waded knee-deep to buy groceries at the store."

"I remember that too."

She laughed. She said, "You're a writer. You're a cheat! You remember everything!"

The rain was like a slender curtain between their veranda and the rest of a saturated world. A fine mist of dampness permeated the air. They could feel it on the rims of the glasses from which they drank and breathed it as a fisherman might breathe in a fog. He said,

"It's strange. It's as though each day of rain is washing away another layer of recent history, exposing forgotten layers of the past ... "

He remembered walking along a beach somewhere in the tropics, with the sea on his right and palm trees on his left. There was no sound at all, no birds either visible or hidden in the foliage, and the sea was as still as a bowl of mercury. Ahead of him, drawn up on the sand so far that it was nearly in the shade of the palm trees, there was a boat, an obviously abandoned boat, in length about thirty foot, barely listing, its stern extending almost halfway to the edge of the sea.

He reached up and ran his fingertips along the gunwale. It had the texture of stippled plaster and contained traces of the original red and blue paint on the crumbling ridges. The name of the boat, once stenciled in black letters, was now too faded and weather-worn to make out, but he intuited, he *knew*, that it was the name of a girl the owner of the boat had loved but had lost while he was out at sea. And then suddenly, as though the curtain had been raised on a vast stage—*no*, as though the curtain had dissolved as he had walked through it—he saw a young woman standing in the shallows, holding up the hem of her dress with one hand and shielding her eyes with the other. The distance between them was no more than twenty feet and yet she seemed very far away. It would have been no more possible to call out to her than to call out to a ship on the horizon, but he remembered an overwhelming urge to speak to her, to be the focus of her attention even if only for a moment or two. Then the memory rippled and faded and he was again alone on a tropical beach next to an abandoned boat that seemed to hold within its timbers all the salt of a thousand days at sea.

He smiled at the memory. He said,

"Would you like another drink?"

"In a minute, when I've finished this one. What were you remembering? You were very far away."

"A boat abandoned on a beach. A girl. But it wasn't like a memory. More like a waking dream."

"Dreams are only shattered memories, put back together by the mad and blind."

The veranda upon which they stood had four steps leading down to a semi-circular patio surrounded by lawn. The lawn was entirely underwater, the grass-blades an expanse of flowering coral, and the rain had covered the patio to the elevation of the first of the steps. She said,

"It's like a swimming pool. When I was a child, I always wanted a swimming pool. I wanted to dive into it wearing a skin-tight one-piece ivory-colored bathing suit. Like on the cover of *Vogue*." She raised the hem of her dress with her left hand and descended the steps. She looked over her shoulder. She said,

"Do you remember?"

"Remember what?"

"When I was reading Holberg's *Subterranean Voyage of Nicholas Klimn* and eating the box of chocolates you'd given me because I'd caught you smiling at some girl on the Auto-Shuttle—"

"I remember the chocolates. I don't remember the girl."

"—and I flattened out the foil that had been wrapped around the crème noisette and used it as a bookmark. And the more I used it and the more flattened it got the more beautiful it became. A sort of meeting point between poetry and spatial physics. Or better still the after-image caused by a combination of Rayographs and driving very fast down Fifth Avenue on a late December afternoon in the pouring sleet and rain. Oh, and incidentally, the girl was memorable, the chocolates were not."

"But you remembered the chocolates."

"But you failed to remember the girl."

He went over to the drinks trolley that was parked just beside the French doors that led back into their villa and poured himself another martini. She said,

"What was I wearing when we first met?"

"We met at a party on Moon-Base Nine."

"That isn't the answer to the question I asked."

"It's the answer to the question that should've come first."

"What was I wearing?"

"You were wearing toreador pants and a white cotton shirt. What was I?"

She thought for a moment and then shook her head. "I can't remember. I remember the gin ran out and the vol-au-vents were cold. I remember it was snowing outside. I remember I went out onto the balcony because someone had given me a brandy and I needed some fresh air. It was the most wonderful, the freshest air I had ever known. I lit a cigarette and almost immediately a snowflake, an absolutely *enormous* snowflake, landed *sssssssss* on the head of the match. I'd never seen such a perfect snowflake before—and haven't since. And while I was smoking the cigarette, I looked over the balcony railing and down at the street. I think we were four maybe five floors up. And although the party wasn't a very wonderful party, in fact it was really rather second-rate, they'd done a fantastic job of setting up an exterior facsimile of Prague and I remember looking down at the tramlines glittering or gleaming or whatever through the cobblestones, and a streetlight illuminating a poster for the Black-Light Theatre, and everything, all of this, seen through a sort of screen of snow, and seen falling *down*, away from one, so that the flakes of snow were spinning *spinning* between oneself and the street. And I remember the exact texture of the cigarette filter between my lips as I saw a man down on the street, he must've stepped off the departing tram, wearing an overcoat with the collar turned up and a hat with a gorgeously swooping brim and surrounded by—"

"By?"

"—by snowflakes. And then he glanced up at where I was standing, smiled a slender smile, and walked in the direction of the Old Town Square. I remember wanting to call out to him or something, I didn't know what, I took the cigarette out of my mouth and was waving it like it was a children's firework toy, and then another star came and sat on the end of my cigarette and went *sssssssss* just like before . . . "

"A star? Don't you mean snowflake?"

" . . . I mean something beautiful and incredible that fell from the sky. Who knows? There is less difference between a snowflake and a star than there is between a man who steps off a tram and glances up at a balcony and a man who stays on the tram and is merely a silhouette in a square of yellow light . . . "

He stepped down just behind her, on the lowest dry step, and handed her a lighted cigarette. She let the hem of her dress fall to receive it and glanced down at the flimsy cotton half-floating half-sinking in the clear martini-colored water. She smiled. She said,

"In the depths of the deepest sea, in depths deeper even than those discerned of by Professor Apollinax or Nicholas Krimn, there exist creatures that unspool their intestines as a faulty film projector might unspool the works of Jean-Luc Godard, leaving behind them a gorgeous phosphorescence, illuminating with celluloid the submarine."

"*Vivre sa vie* with Anna Karina."

"*The Oval Portrait* by Edgar A. Poe."

"Where did we meet—the second time?"

"In a taxi we shared by sheer coincidence."

"From where to where?"

"From somewhere in the Village to East Fifty-third Street."

"What was I wearing? Can you remember?"

"A black polo-neck sweater and a pair of green-tinted spectacles."

"Can you remember if it was raining or snowing?"

"It was neither, it was eternally spring."

She remembered sitting on a sun-lounger beside a swimming pool. She wore a gold lamé one-piece swimsuit that gave the impression, was *meant* to give the impression, of freshly applied paint. Her long blonde hair was tied up in a bandana and she wore sunglasses with exaggerated white frames. On the table beside her there was a strawberry-colored cocktail in a tall glass and a box of Sobranie cigarettes and an imitation vintage copy of *Harper's Bazaar.* Suddenly there was a small commotion. Three young men wearing swimming trunks had danced, leapt and run across the terrace and jumped into the pool. They resurfaced laughing, plashing the surface of the water, shaking their heads so it was like they gave off sparks. She recognized them, as much by intuition as knowledge, as members of an acrobatic dance company that was staying in the hotel. She thought, They are the happiest people I have ever seen. It is impossible to see them without feeling happy oneself. Tonight I shall make love to all of them or none of them because to separate them would break the structure of a tableau that has taken hours of rehearsal to create. She smiled because it was impossible not to be happy. She took a sip of the cocktail and lit a slender blue Sobranie cigarette.

She smiled at the memory. She said,

"You once bought me a bouquet of flowers and in the middle of the bouquet was a rose."

"Yes, I remember."

"Oh, surely not! I've always loved the way you buy me flowers when there isn't any necessity, I mean apart from a birthday or an anniversary or even an apology. It's wonderfully *you.* But the bouquet to which I'm referring . . . "

"But I do remember . . . "

"Oh, darling, you must've bought me dozens—no, *hundreds*—of bouquets in the last ten years. I'm talking about a very *specific* bouquet. A bouquet of mixed summertime flowers in the middle of which was a single orange rose. If it had been a green rose or a blue rose . . . "

"It wasn't. It wasn't green or blue. It was orange."

"It was orange because I just *told* you it was orange. Oh, if I asked if you remembered, it wasn't a proper question, just a figure of speech . . . "

"But I *do* remember."

"What do you—no, *how* do you—remember?"

"Because the bouquet was too large to fit in a single vase, so you divided it into two. The vase containing the rose—"

"The orange rose . . . "

"—you placed on the bathroom windowsill. Our bathroom was—still is—all white: white walls, white ceiling, white sanitation chamber, white windowsill. But every day for at least a week there was this incredibly beautiful orange rose, almost like some kind of totemic sun, against this background of totalitarian—*white*. And each day, of course, it expanded, opened out, and seemed—"

"And seemed?"

"—extraordinarily *excited*. For what reason, exactly, I have never known, but I don't think there has ever been—well, if not a day, at least a week—when I haven't remembered that rose and thought about it. The contrast. Not just between the rose and the bathroom, but between the rose and the bathroom and myself."

"Now *I* remember. I used to sanitate naked and imagine my skin was becoming the petals of the rose. And when I stepped out of the sanitation chamber—"

"You believed for one moment of passionate empathy that you and the rose had become one."

"I truly believed. And when we made love, I tore you to pieces with my fingernails because my fingernails had become thorns. And when we lay apart the sweat on my skin had become the dew on the petals of a rose. And when I died on the bathroom windowsill—"

"When you died . . . "

"—I was reincarnated as someone the same, but *not* the same. As some new version, like a composer's variation on a theme. I cracked and peeled and flayed myself, and the sound I made was like walking over pebbles on a beach and at the same time peeling a strip of sellotape off a sheet of glass. I was realized as metal and silver and glistened like the underside of the lid on a jar of honey when the jar is new. Do you remember?"

"One cannot remember what one never knew. I remember the dead petals on the bathroom windowsill. I remember the texture of them in the palm of my hand. I remember the long lacerations and the curling wood-shavings of skin when we made love. But memory is a genie that constantly reshapes its own bottle. Indeed, I often wonder where memory ends and fiction begins . . . "

It had rained for nine days. The color had long ago bleached out of the world and the cupolas and the domes and the rooftops were pewter-gray. Even the sky was saturated, and rippled in the breeze like a photograph in a developing tray. She said,

"The taxi driver turned left instead of right. A blind alley. Sheets of newspaper blowing around the fire-escapes. A cat with enormous yellow eyes caught in the headlamps. A woman's scream coming from an upstairs window. A slamming casement. A sound of breaking glass."

"Where did we end up?"

"In a bar on the waterfront. In a bar that catered solely for fishermen and longshoremen and all the rough types of women that rely on both. A bar divided from the sea by an all-pervading smothering jungle of masts and spars and impenetrable fog. A bar where, when the door swung open, all the ghosts of the dead and the drowned crammed like a sickening mist through the aperture, small wisps of them, that might've been fingers or toes, trickling across the spit-stained beer-stained wooden floor."

"I remember. I wore a white roll-necked sweater and a jacket with brass buttons. I was sitting next to a Chinaman who was drinking bourbon and smoking a marijuana cigarette. The bartender had J E S U S tattooed across the fingers of his right hand and S A T A N tattooed across the fingers of his left. I remember an atmosphere of permanent dampness and suppressed violence and hopeless grief."

"I remember the foghorn. In fact, that's *all* I remember. What are those birds that fly by night over the ocean?"

"Albatrosses?"

"No. Well, maybe they do, but those aren't the birds I'm thinking of. I imagined I was one of those birds in silent passage over an unknown sea, guided only by a lozenge of amber-colored light shining dimly through the mist and the sound of a foghorn reminding me that I was close to land."

"Frigate birds?"

"That's right, thank you. Frigate birds. Now I remember. They can fly for weeks, alone in the darkness of the night and then alone above an empty sunlit sea."

"There is a film where they run through The Louvre in Paris."

"There is a novel where they steal a painting called *The Rhinoceros* from The National Gallery in London."

They were silent for a moment, their soundtrack only the steady white noise of the rain. She said,

"There are birds called frigate birds ... What was I wearing when we first met?"

"You were wearing toreador pants and a white cotton shirt. And a pearl on a thin gold chain between the oyster of your breasts."

"I remember now. I remember everything. I remember climbing out of a yellow taxi and entering a tall building. I remember looking up and seeing story upon story of galleries, voices echoing, and rows upon rows of expressionless faces looking down. Awful faces, disturbing faces, faces without noses or mouths or eyes, but still those voices, those echoing voices, passing some kind of judgment, issuing some kind of sentence in response to an unspecified crime."

"I remember everything too. Except what we talked about before the rain."

He flicked his cigarette away and put his hand on her shoulder. The cotton of her dress was damp and revealed the strap of her brassiere. She shivered and placed her own free hand on his. She said,

"Now, if there is any truth in any legend at all, the dead will arise from the sea and reclaim their presence on the land. Bedraggled and fish-blinded, trailing seaweed, their thigh-high boots oozing with—"

"Mud and foul water?"

"—and spilling shoals of whitebait from the holes that pirates made. Do you see them yet?"

"I think I do."

Together they watched the reanimated sailors of a distant past walk towards them through successive sheets of rain. The woman was strikingly beautiful and the man simultaneously elegant and handsome, and the contrast between themselves and that which approached was almost like a curtain of static electricity through which neither they nor their submarine visitors could pass. Together they watched the shades of ancient shipwrecks fade into an endless ocean of rain.

•

Harry sat down beside me, the gun on his lap. He said,

"Hey, kiddo."

"Uh, huh."

"Nobody's breathing out here except us."

I looked along the shore and saw Billy Ray laid out on the sand, his feet facing the ocean, a bottle of beer still upright in his outstretched hand. Eight-Ball had disappeared behind a couple of old rowboats drawn up on the beach. They had been overturned and, in the uneasy half-light of early morning, resembled strange creatures washed up by a storm. I said,

"I hate it when the night's over but the day won't start."

In the forty or so minutes since we drove onto the beach the sea had changed from purple to red to an urgent cobalt blue. The sun, however, had stubbornly refused to rise and was caught between the green horizon and the orange sky like a buoy with horizontal blue and yellow stripes stuck in a slick of tar. Or a balloon, I thought, with too much weight in its basket that can't get above the rooftops. I took a pack of Luckies out of my shirt pocket and Harry took one and I took one and then Harry went around the back of the car and got us two more beers. He had a bottle-opener on his key ring. He said,

"How 'bout we drive down to Slatz' Diner, get some breakfast? Bacon and eggs and home fries. Coffee and cold beer."

"Okay."

Harry handed me his beer bottle while he was reversing. He swung the wheel over and looked up in the rear-view mirror. He caught my eye. He said,

"I wouldn't worry 'bout Billy Ray nor Eight-Ball."

"I wasn't."

We weren't. Harry's 1958 Thunderbird turned off the beach and back onto the road. The sky in the rear-view mirror glowed a kind of sick feverish orange. I lit a cigarette and rolled down the passenger-side window and watched the sun stuck in the ocean get smaller and smaller until it was too small to see.

# Like a Lizard
# on White Plaster

S he sat at the dressing table of their hotel room in Havana, painting her fingernails alternate shades of green—the harsh green that painters call viridian and a shimmering tropical version by Maybelline containing flecks of gold. She held her hand palm outwards, the elbow bent at forty-five degrees, applying the tiny brush with the delicacy of a Chinese artist. The mirror of the dressing table reflected the room behind her, principally the bed, upon which a man wearing a polo shirt and a pair of khaki shorts was sitting up and reading a Cuban newspaper. On the bedside table there was a portable typewriter out of its case and a glass of white rum. The tall louvered doors that led out onto the balcony were open and the sound of guaracha music from the radio in a street-level café mingled with the noise of motorcycles and people's raised voices and sudden bursts of competing music from open-topped American cars. She flexed the fingers of her right hand and replaced the brush in the top of the shimmer-green varnish bottle with the thumb and the middle-finger of her left, the remaining three outstretched as in a Peking opera. She stood up and went out onto the balcony. It was already late morning and across the bay the white facades of Casablanca shone with a fierce, clean whiteness that contrasted beautifully with the blue of the sea and made a neat backdrop for her own outfit, a white blouse and a pair of navy-blue slacks. She thought, How strange it all seems. Everywhere you go there's somewhere the same, but not the same. Last year we were in Casablanca in North Africa, and now I'm looking at Casablanca in the Caribbean, and only a few months ago we were in Shanghai for that modeling assignment, and last night we ate beef in oyster sauce in the Barrio Chino. She closed her eyes against the brightness and retained an after-image of the sunlight sparkling on the surface of the sea. She opened them again and glanced down at her slacks and thought, I have a green pair in the wardrobe that will look better with these fingernails, and went back into the hotel room. It seemed suddenly wonderfully cool, subaquatic almost, after being outside. She said,

"Darling?"

"Uh-huh?"

"Tell me what you think."

He let down one side of the newspaper and looked at where she wanted him to look. She had spread out the fingers of her right hand and placed that hand against the wall between the balcony and the dressing table. She said,

"Well?"

He narrowed his eyes ever so slightly, hesitated no more than half a second, and said,

"Like a lizard on white plaster. Like a lizard basking in the sun on a white plaster wall."

She felt deflated. It was a beautiful phrase that had taken him no time to think of and nearly no effort to say. And now he had straightened up the paper and was reading again. He hadn't even glanced at the typewriter, as though it, the image of the lizard, as though she, were not worth writing down. She removed her hand and blew gently on the still-wet nails. When they were dry, she would change her slacks for another pair, a green pair, or better still a matching skirt, and go down to the café where they were playing guaracha music and order a bottle of ice-cold Cacique beer—

"Cacique cerveza hielo frio, por favor!"

—and then later take the ferry to Casablanca and put her hands against its radiant white walls and feel the sun's warmth stored in the ancient stone transfer itself through the palms of her hands and invite people to admire the two lizards, viridian green and green with flecks of gold, basking in the North African sun . . .

Later, when her nails were fully dry. She would do so many wonderful things when her nails were dry.

# The Girl Boutique

I n the bed in the bedroom of the apartment on Xiaoping Lu, Xin Pu Wang, with customary reluctance, opened his eyes.

*c-lick*

In the bed in the bedroom of the apartment on Xiaoping Lu, Xin Pu Wang, with customary reluctance, opened his eyes and, through a narrow aperture between pillow and duvet, saw his wife, Hong Ma, walk left and right, visible only from the shoulder to the waist, firstly wearing an oyster-colored brassiere

*c-lick*

and then, a minute later, passing again through his abbreviated line of sight, maneuvering her left arm into the sleeve of a cream silk blouse.

*c-lick c-lick*

No sooner, however, had she disappeared than she reappeared, facing the bed as she deftly buttoned the blouse up to an invisible neck, doing so with an attitude of disdain as palpable as the material of the pillow against his cheek. He felt her eyes boring through the duvet, her perfectly-painted scarlet fingernails hovering above the top button

*c-lick*

before she turned and disappeared for the last time, her tangible presence now reduced to the noise of high heels on the wooden floor and finally the emphatic closure of the apartment door

*c-lack c-lack, c-lack c-lack, c-lack c-lack*

*SLAM!*

while in the bed in the bedroom of the apartment on Xiaoping Lu, Xin Pu Wang turned over to face the wall and once again closed his eyes.

•

Xin Pu Wang spent the majority of his days either walking or cycling around the backstreets of Shenyang, taking photographs with a Zenit camera. One day he went into one of the noodle shops on the food street near the Qing Dynasty palaces and said,

"I am the loneliest married man in Liaoning Province. I have no job, my wife openly disrespects me, and nobody will publish my photographs."

The proprietor, who was very old, came to his table. He said,

"Good morning to you too, young fellow. What will you have?"

"A bowl of spiced noodles," replied Xin Pu Wang, "with pork and bean shoots."

"It is our specialty," said the old man. He seemed very happy. He walked unsteadily between the rough-hewn cigarette-burned wooden tables as one might walk on the deck of a ship, holding the backs of chairs for support. He called out the order to a chef somewhere out of sight. Xin Pu Wang took a photograph of the interior of the shop—

### *c-lick FLASH!*

The light was wrong, but it didn't matter. A little of the old man's happiness had rubbed off on him. It was worth recording.

•

One day Xin Pu Wang returned home to find that his wife had, during his absence, been in, got changed, and gone out again. The reason he knew was that her original underwear had been cast on the bed and the blouse and skirt he had (through the narrow aperture between pillow and duvet) seen her put on only a couple of hours earlier were suspended from a hanger which was itself suspended from the outside of the wardrobe door. Why had she changed her mind (and her clothes)? Frankly, he neither knew nor cared. But what struck him with a sudden and extraordinary force was this—

The items of underwear on the bed had been thrown down in such a way that (certainly by accident, not design) brassiere, panties, suspender belt and stockings were not just facing up but also in exact spatial proportion as though being worn by an invisible woman. Xin Pu Wang felt an overwhelming sense of discovery. The stocking that would have been (that was?) on the right leg was draped over the end of the bed in such a way as to give the impression of 3-D. Not only *that*, but the stocking that would have been (that was?) on the left leg was bent at the knee in such a way as to be intensely, almost wantonly, seductive. Xin Pu Wang, the Zenit still slung around his neck, sat down very slowly on the stool that matched Hong Ma's dressing table. He stayed sitting there for some time.

•

Every day for the next two weeks Xin Pu Wang only briefly patrolled the streets looking for photographs before returning home and arranging—rearranging—Hong Ma's underwear in such a way as to represent

### What?

What indeed? Xin Pu Wang would undress to his white Y-front underpants and sit on the corner of the bed. How long he sat there he never exactly knew, but every so often, at intervals of maybe three or four minutes, he would allow himself a sideways glance. It had the same feeling as when he had stolen a glance at the strikingly pretty girl in middle school three desks away. One morning, down in the courtyard, a knife-grinder in a three-wheeled motorized cart could be heard advertising his services through a tin megaphone

## MO JIAN ZI LEI—QIANG CAI DAO

and what had always previously seemed like a harsh and intrusive noise became, on this occasion, strangely soothing. The imaginary woman on the bed (wearing, on this bright December morning, a black under-wired bra, matching panties, nearly-sheer charcoal-gray stockings and—oh, recent inspiration!—a pair of lacy costume gloves bought for some party Hong Ma had attended years before) smiled in her sleep. For the first time since this—romance?—had begun, Xin Pu Wang felt ashamed of the erection that distorted the cheap cotton fabric of his own underwear. He very carefully removed himself from the bed (so as not to disturb her) and put his penis under the cold tap in the bathroom. The knife-grinder could still be heard (albeit faintly) in the courtyard of the neighboring apartment block. Xin Pu Wang turned his head to the window to listen.

# MO JIAN ZI LEI—QIANG CAI DAO

He turned off the tap.

•

After an hour or so Xin Pu Wang would resume his wanderings, on foot or by bicycle, the Zenit slung around his neck, through the backstreets and alleyways of the city, usually ending up at the noodle shop on the food street near the Qing Dynasty palaces

陈氏四季面条

where he was recognized and greeted by the proprietor, Mr. Chen,

## CHEN'S FOUR SEASONS NOODLES

who would bring him a laminated cardboard menu and then, not bothering to wait for an order, turn to the kitchen-end to shout for spicy noodles with pork and bean-shoots. Xin Pu Wang said,

"When I first came here, I was the loneliest married man in Liaoning Province. I had no job, my wife openly disrespected me, and nobody would publish my photographs."

"That is reasonable," said Mr. Chen.

"Now," continued Xin Pu Wang, "I am dreaming only of my new-found imaginary love. I am sincerely happy. Thank you."

"Thank you?"

"Thank you. I might have committed suicide in your restaurant," he hesitated, "had you not been so kind."

"It is our specialty," said the old man. He seemed very happy. He took a packet of cigarettes out of the pocket of his shirt. He said,

"Come again, please. We are seldom not open."

and returned to his counter, using chair-backs for support, the counter behind which were shelves containing bottles of Chinese alcohol in red and gold boxes, in blue and gold boxes, and in boxes of red and blue and gold.

*c-lick FLASH!*

One day, returning home from Mr. Chen's, Xin Pu Wang did a double-take as he walked past a row of small shops

*c-lick rewind c-lick*

and saw the mannequin in one of the windows.

*rewind c-lick FLASH!*

The name of the shop was written in Chinese

王氏时装

and in English

# WANG'S GIRL BOUTIQUE

and was set back from the pavement down a small flight of concrete steps. Xin Pu Wang, strangely light-headed, descended from street-level, treading carefully on the icy concrete and aware, for the first time, that the laces in his shoes were mismatched, the left-side pair a noticeably different shade of brown from the right. He stood in front of the window. The light was poor but the mannequin was still beautiful. He pushed open the glass door and was greeted by a gold-painted plastic teddy bear on a mock-Grecian plinth that said, "Ni hao!" A woman, small, rather plump, with elaborate hair that she patted with the palm of her hand, appeared from behind a counter towards the rear of the shop. Her blouse was a cheap shiny man-made material that Hong Ma would not have been seen dead in, but she had a kind face and her smile of welcome was genuine rather than professional. She said,

"May I help you?"

Xin Pu Wang opened his mouth to say something polite but all that came out was:

"How much?"

"How—?" The saleswoman followed his gaze. She said,

"Oh, you mean—Yes. The hat? Forty-five yuan. The blouse, thirty."

"No. Everything."

"Everything? Skirt, sixty. Belt, twenty. Shoes, one-oh-five. Ten percent discount if you buy two or more." A brief pause. "Fifteen for cash."

She smiled. She was obviously in need of customers. He said (with a calmness that surprised him),

"You misunderstand. I mean, I don't just want the clothes. I mean, yes, I do want the clothes. But I also want the lady wearing them."

There was a silence, a very *tangible* silence, while the saleswoman processed what she had heard. She said, "Let me fetch the manager," and departed with a brief glance over her shoulder. The mannequin gave Xin Pu Wang a beautiful smile then immediately straightened her face as the manager appeared from an office somewhere out back. His attitude combined curiosity with annoyance and he was smoking a cigarette. Xin Pu Wang explained what he wanted. The manager's initial curiosity was swiftly replaced by an attitude of casual disrespect. He said,

"Nine hundred. For everything. Including the clothes."

He looked at his cigarette. He tapped off a cue-tip of ash. It made a small *plash* on the white-tiled floor. He smeared the toe of his shoe over it. He looked up at Xin Pu Wang. He said,

"It's a good offer. You won't find better elsewhere. Song Wei?"

The saleswoman, previously so nice, now seemed embarrassed and was occupying herself with making tidy a rail of fake-fur coats. She stopped what she was doing and patted her hair with the palm of her hand. She said,

"True, Mr. Zhang. Very reasonable."

and glanced briefly and uncomfortably at Xin Pu Wang.

The manager, Mr. Zhang, looked down at the smear of cigarette ash on the floor and Zorro-zedded it with the toe of his shoe. He glanced back up. He said,

"Well?"

and there was silence for two maybe three seconds. Then:

"You will have it by this time tomorrow," said Xin Pu Wang, hardly aware of the actual tangible reality of the (grossly inflated) sum, "and please accept this as surety. It is worth quite as much." He maneuvered the camera strap over his head and handed the Zenit to the manager. He turned to the saleswoman, Song Wei. He said,

"And thank you so much. You have been sincerely kind. You remind me," he smiled a shy smile, "of a friend of mine, Mr. Chen."

The battery-operated plastic teddy bear that said Ni hao! said "Ni hao!" as Xin Pu Wang pushed open the glass door of the boutique and stepped out onto the ice-hardened, breath-freezing January streets of Shenyang.

Xin Pu Wang arrived home to an empty apartment. He automatically unslung the Zenit from around his neck and seemed mildly surprised it wasn't there to unsling. He went on through to the bedroom and sat down on the bed next to that morning's arrangement of bra, panties and tights. The bra was red, the panties black, the tights semi-sheer with a bluish sheen. With a small shudder he brushed them aside—almost immediately (and a little guiltily) re-smoothing the tights where they had become ruched over an imaginary thigh. The low winter sun came through the window blinds in flimsy sheets grained with dust. Xin Pu Wang touched the cup of the bra where it joined the strap, then ran his hand along the strap until it curved underneath an imaginary back. At first, he was not even aware that he was crying

*c-lick*

—at least not until he was conscious of the tickly sensation of tears on the side of his nose

*c-lick SPLASH!*

and whether or not he was *entirely* aware of it even then we cannot possibly know.

*rewind SPLASH! c-lick SPLASH! c-lick SPLASH!*

•

Outside, in the ice-hardened courtyard, nineteen sheer stories below, the small crowd that always gathers around an incident having reluctantly dispersed, a knife grinder advertised his presence through a battery-operated tin megaphone

## MO JIAN ZI LEI—QIANG CAI DAO

and on the food street near the Qing Dynasty palaces Mr. Chen steadied himself between two rows of cigarette-burned wooden tables

*c-lick*

and wiped a laminated menu for spicy noodles with a damp cloth

*s-lick c-lick FLASH!*

while in the office of Wang's Girl Boutique the manager, Mr. Zhang, smoked a cigarette and looked disdainfully at the Zenit camera that made a clunky ornament on an otherwise uncluttered desk.

*c-lick FLASH!*

•

When Hong Ma returned home in the early evening, the apartment was ridiculously, almost icebox cold. She wrenched down the casement of the living room window

*c-lick SLAM!*

and proceeded into the bedroom, muttering curses under her nearly visible breath. Items of underwear she recognized as her own were bizarrely arranged on the bed's counterpane. A blouse and skirt were hanging from a wire coat hanger on the outside of the bedroom wardrobe, and Hong Ma glanced at them briefly before releasing the bamboo slats of the window blind

*shutter-shutter slapper-slapper shutter-shutter slap-shut SLAT!*

and switching on the electric overhead light. She took a critical look around the room before dumping her Daphne shoulder bag on the bed and kicking off her shoes. She removed her ear-rings and clinked them down on the glass-topped dressing table. She went into the bathroom and turned on the shower. She came back into the bedroom. She undid the pins from her hair. She undressed. She unhitched her brassiere. She unpeeled her stockings. She removed her panties. She dropped everything in a jumbled heap on the bedroom floor. She glanced at herself in the mirror, tilting her head sideways and touching the side of her cheek. She shivered. She left the door of the bathroom open and entered the shower.

## *c-lick FLASH!*

# The Undead

In the evenings he read by the light of an oil lamp while the girl he lived with brushed her hair. Sometimes a breeze blew in through the unglazed windows and made the flame dance higher or lean sideways and the shape of the pages changed and the words on the pages were not the same. Other times it rained and the noise of the rain made reading impossible, but always in the mornings the hut in the jungle near the sea was at peacefulness and you could hear the quick scratching sound of geckos among the roof supports and the occasional deep vibrating croak of a monitor lizard that lived somewhere behind the open-sided wooden structure that made an improvised shower. The monitor lizard they had never seen, but from the size of its voice was unusually large and was perhaps the reason that there had never been a rat or a snake in the vicinity of the hut. There was a clearing made of hard-packed sandy earth where the hut was located, surrounded by trees, and the boy set up a banana box as a table next to a twisted tree branch as a stool and put his typewriter on the banana box. The boy wrote well but typed badly and sound of the typewriter was loud and deliberate and well-spaced like the beginning or the end of the rain. The rain fell randomly rather than according to a season and the hut in the jungle was near the sea but was hidden from it by the trees.

•

The boy had arrived on a ship from America by way of the Andaman Islands and the girl had been sitting under a palm tree, looking out at the sea.

•

In the fall, after a prolonged period of dry weather, a period when the sky was filled with rain clouds every morning but the clouds passed over in less than an hour and released their rain over the mountains far from the sea, he became sick and for many days it seemed like he would die. He didn't die, but he became very pale underneath his tan and very weak and twice collapsed on his way to the open-sided wooden structure that made an improvised shower. He lay with his face against the hard-packed sandy earth and everything that was very small seemed very big and he could see the different colors and the different facets of every grain of sand and the lunar craters that had been made by drops of water from when the girl had washed her hair. He lay in the clearing where the hut was located and the monitor lizard made its croaking valediction from behind the trees.

•

Even when the worst was over he became tired very easily and the light of the oil lamp hurt his eyes. He lay on the bed in the hut in the darkness and watched the shapes of the trees through the unglazed windows and sometimes he remembered the shapes of the sea when he dropped himself off the deck of the freighter, staying under for as long as he was able, fearful of surfacing in a beam of light, and sometimes he dreamed he was falling through the tree branches, desperately wanting them to break his fall, but always he woke up choking and gasping and the girl was beside him, holding a bowl of water for him to drink from, and then arak in a small wooden cup. She said,

"My nenek had a fetish boneka—you understand? A jelangkung. It was very black and very ugly and it lived in a box—"

"A box?"

"—made of wood carved from the tamarind tree. My nenek was a bad woman, a penyihir, and the day she died, I was twelve years old, I took the doll out of its box and threw it into the sea. But the night of the next moon it returned and so I took it outside and buried it under a banana tree. The bananas turned black and fell down and the banana tree died and the boneka returned again and I was only angry now and not afraid. Maybe good wisdom is learned from bad, and so I took the doll, the evil fetish doll, to the market in the town and sold it for fifty thousand rupiah to a tourist from Holland. He thought he had such a bargain from a simple village girl but I smiled and pretended I was excited to see all this money and so he went away to a bus where other tourists were waiting, very happy and very red and smelling of sweat and sun-tan oil. He smiled at me through the window of the bus when it drove away and held up the boneka and pointed at it with his other hand and then waved. Then there were children running after the bus and men on bicycles holding up mangoes and coconuts and strings of beads and then a lot of dust and the Dutchman and my nenek's doll disappeared . . . "

"Disappeared?"

"Oh, yes. When the Dutch take something from Indonesia it is *very* hard to get it back. All nenek's evil spirits never took account of *that* . . . " She smiled. She said,

"I am only happy to meet a man who believes in love but does not believe in ghosts. Who loves me ... " She went suddenly quiet and turned away her face. She said,

"Who allows me to love him. And maybe loves me a little in return ... "

But when she looked back he was sleeping. The candle she had lit in place of the oil lamp made different shadows across his chest and face and the arak cup had rolled away from his hand that hung beside the bed. He was breathing normally and his face in the last of the candlelight before she exhaled it out was even more beautiful than the sea.

•

"Where you from?"

"America."

"Yo, man, we's *all* from Amer-i-ka. I mean, where's *in* America you from?"

"Chicago." Then: "And you?"

"Dominican Republic, by way of Orange, New Jersey. By way of In-do-*ne*-sia." The black man moved closer and put his mouth to the white man's ear. He said,

"How bad you get it?"

"Bad enough. Not so bad."

"Anything broken? Broken so's you can't swim, I mean."

"No."

"Good. Now, listen—pirate ships is pirate rules. I *like* you, but I don't *die* for you. Understand?"

"I understand."

"Good. Because when you hit the water you stay under and then you *swim*, you understand?"

"Uh, huh."

"Uh, huh. These people has superstition up to their *eye*balls, man, an' I don't intend to be one of their *ghosts* ... "

•

They lay in the dark one night, when the wind and the rain had blown the candles out, and the girl told him about Babi Ngopet, the man who can turn himself into a pig, and Tuyul, the hairless child-ghost, who steals money from you when you sleep—and will even steal the milk from a mother's breast. She said,

"Then there is Sundel Bolong who is also named Kuntilanak."

"Kuntilanak." He repeated the word as though to remember it. She said, "Yes, Kuntilanak. The ghost with a hole in her stomach where there was once a child. Kuntilanak, who tore the conception of rape from inside herself and died but did not die, and who walks in limbo through the jungle and who hates all men." She saw that the rain had stopped and the wind had become a breeze and lit two candles on a shelf above their bed. She said, "And there is too Pocong—"

"Pocong?"

"—who is a woman also, wronged how but I cannot recall. She is wrapped all in white, only her face is showing, and she is a warning of bad things. If you see her, you will sicken." She hesitated. She said, "I nearly believed . . ."

"Believed?"

" . . . believed. Believed that when you, you, my tuan, became sick it was because you had seen Pocong. The night you left me to sit in the moonlight and look at the sea. And the following morning was the beginning of how you nearly died."

There was a rustle in the rafters of geckos made active by the light. He laughed. He said,

"I saw nobody, not even a ghost."

But behind the laughter and to himself he said: I saw everything again as though it were through the mirror of the sea. I saw the water more black than I thought could be possible and, twenty feet to my right, the man from Santo Domingo by way of New Jersey caught in the pitiless phosphorescence of the ship's searchlight, the shouts from high up on the deck, the *crack-cerack* of gunfire, the sheer immediate panic of another dive, the appalling eternal suffocating blackness of the midnight sea. The fear of total oblivion. The sound of a thousand machines in your ears. He reached out and touched her cheek with his fingertips. He said,

"Not even a ghost."

•

"I shall not wear a green dress for you, however well you love me."

"Because you fear snakes?"

"No. Because I fear Nyirorokidul."

He lay on a hammock they had rigged up between two trees and smoked a cigarette and looked at the sunlight on the leaves through the tattered brim of an old straw hat. He said,

"One day I shall write down all these stories. Not one day, in fact, but very soon. When I'm not so damn tired I can't stay awake more than half an hour. When I can stand to hear the racket the typewriter makes. Who is—? I'm sorry—"

"Nyirorokidul? She is a Javanese princess, the daughter of the King of Keraton, rich, beautiful and—*sombong*. I do not know the English word. It means she thinks herself very superior, very *high* . . ."

The boy exhaled a plume of cigarette smoke from beneath the brim of his hat. He said,

"Maybe haughty, maybe proud. She thinks she is very superior to you and me."

"She *thinks*, but she is not. Neither alive nor dead, but somewhere in-between. And always she is wearing a green dress and always is madly jealous of another girl wearing color the same. So—" She paused and looked at where the trees hid their clearing from the sea.

"So?"

"—*So*, she comes to the beach at night and steals away women or girls who are wearing green, leading them out into the sea until they drown. Offerings, sesajen, are left on the shore and you will see them floating on the surface of the sea. But they cannot bring back the dead. *They* will become ghosts under a banana tree . . ." She smiled. She said, "It is strange to talk of ghosts in sunlight. I should rather cook rice with some coconut milk and the eggs I bought yesterday." She looked away. She said, "I would rather make love to you. Because that is strange in sunlight too."

A bird came suddenly with a *crash* and a *flap*, like a blue and green and red and yellow ceiling fan—*c-rash flapper-flapper-flapper-flap*—caught in the branches of the trees that screened their clearing from the sea.

•

He trod water, watching for the searchlight out of the corner of his eye, plunging himself under the surface as the sweep of light and the *rat-a-tat-a-tat-a-tat* of machine guns turned the sea into a box of knives.

•

He became well again, this boy, and resumed his habit of fishing in the early mornings and then typewriting until the sun said that it was time to drink beer. But sometimes he would walk with the girl to the local market, there to buy rice and eggs and chicken and corn, and then hire two motorcycle taxis, one for him, one for her, each driver racing the other along the nearly-impossible un-surfaced road, their passengers shouting encouragement and mock-insults in equal measure, the squawking and gibbering of the birds and the monkeys and the other tree-dwellers only adding to the madness and confusion as the motorbikes, the *ojeks*, slewed and fish-tailed around corners, the boy and the girl simultaneously laughing and screaming like kids on the ghost train at Coney Island. He said (he shouted) when they more or less drew abreast,

"Hey, you cheated when you gave me the eggs!"

"Our mangoes we carry weigh fifty times!"

"I still say it's a bloody disadvantage!"

"Good! We have like on horses a *han-di-cap!*"

And afterwards swimming to wash the dust from their hair and their faces. And afterwards walking through the thin screen of jungle that separated the clearing where their hut was located from the sea.

•

"Tell me about this ghost train, this hantu kereta. Tell me about this Coney Island. Tell me *everything*, tuan. For example, is it true that American girls use ice-cream instead of coconut oil? To make their hair shiny like Audrey Hepburn, Marilyn Monroe?"

"Use *what?*"

She hesitated. She said, "Es krim?"

He laughed and then she laughed also and they drank another glass of the local arak and he touched the corner of her left eye with the middle finger of his right hand and ran it down over the curve of her cheek-bone to the corner of her mouth. Then he rolled away from her and lay on his back and lit a cigarette and looked up at the thatch of the ceiling where the geckos rustled and skittered. He said,

"Tell me again about all the ghosts I forgot when I was too weak to remember. There was the one I hated the most, the one who was like some sick version of a baby."

"Tuyul."

"Tuyul. And the one with the hole in her chest."

"Kuntilanak."

"Kuntilanak." He said it slowly. Kun-*til*-a-nak. He breathed out a plume of smoke. He said, "And the one, the princess, to do with a green dress."

"Nyirorokidul."

The blue haze of his cigarette smoke floated underneath the cross-beams of the ceiling. He reached out his hand and touched her again. He said,

"I remember. They leave offerings of flowers on the beach and the tide comes in and carries them out to sea." He caught the swift motion of a gecko between two blades of palm-tree thatch, the sudden reciprocal glance of an eye. He said,

"I am more scared of people than of ghosts."

•

They lost track of the months, never mind the days, so they did not know that it was exactly one year since he had arrived on the beach where she was sitting, watching the sun rise over the level of the sea. But although they did not know with the knowledge one might obtain from a calendar or a newspaper, they were somehow aware that a certain span of time had elapsed that was significant, and they were self-conscious with each other and they listened for the scrabbling scurry of geckos in the roof thatch to break the silence as a couple in New York might, as a substitute for conversation, listen for the sound of traffic drifting up from the street. It passed, this awkwardness, but the noise of the boy's typewriter became steadier and more controlled, and the hours he kept, even the arak and cigarette breaks he observed, were more regular and there was more then a sense of the clearing in the jungle being organized—like home. At last he said, the boy said,

"I have written all the stories you told me, but on paper they are flat and lifeless, whereas when you spoke them to me . . . " He took a deep pull on his cigarette and blew the smoke out towards the trees. "Maybe that's how it is. Maybe every ghost story you've ever read is just a real story's shadow on the wall of a cave." He looked at the girl and smiled. He said,

"Never mind. They are my souvenir. My insurance against the day when I will have forgotten how to say Nyirorokidul."

"And Kuntilanak. That you must remember too." The girl smiled also, but the knowledge of the meaning of what he had said made everything stop and become dark for the space of two seconds, leaving pinpricks of light in front of her eyes. She said,

"I have made rice with eggs to go with the fish you caught this morning. And there is the man who sells from an ojek beer Bintang cold. But I wish I had a gun to shoot the macaque that stole our pineapple. *Him* I will teach the meaning of respect for hantu." She clicked her fingers and laughed. She said,

"Tomorrow at dawn I will wait again for a foreign boy to swim home from the sea. Laki-laki asing. And then maybe a new story. I have never told you of Malin Kundang."

He examined the tip of his cigarette. He said,

"I am filled with stories. And something now I understand—" He took a final draw and then flicked the cigarette in the direction of the trees. "If there are only a handful of stories, they must not be written down. Because each time they are told they become different from before." And then he smiled, his old smile, the one that was more beautiful than a mango sliced on a banana leaf. He said,

"Let us drink that beer while it remains cold."

•

Down, down, down through the depths, through the ink-purple mussel-black strata of the sea, an endless agonizing slow-motion falling, and then the burst of illumination, the sense of becoming one with infinity, an enlightenment vouchsafed to few—few, at least, save holy men on Chinese mountain tops; and finally an after-image of the stars left behind, an after-image revealed as the pin-prick phosphorescent sensors of a thousand grotesque and nameless inhabitants of the ultra-deep . . .

And there, in the aperture of that vast funnel of descent, backlit by the searchlight of a pirate ship, arms hands in an outspread gesture of futile supplication, the big black man floating silently face-down on the surface of the sea . . .

•

He still had the pair of trousers he had worn when he arrived from the sea and these trousers he now wore again when he went to go fishing. Often now he went fishing before the sun had risen and he came back bearing not just a string of six or seven fish but also an aura of aloneness that corresponded to the way his bare feet left no imprint on the hard-packed sandy earth that separated their hut from the jungle that screened them from the sea. The girl would be in the makeshift shower or else newly come out of it and drying her hair and the boy would pass her with the fish suspended from a pole over his shoulder and the macaque would chatter and screech from behind the foliage of the trees. But then, not many minutes later, the boy would reappear with the fish filleted and ready to be roasted on a fire that the girl would make and he would smile and take a cigarette from the packet she offered him and kiss her with the delicate shyness of when he first arrived from the sea. And he would pour himself a bottle of Bintang bir dingin and she would say,

"Last night I remembered that story I have not yet told you, the story of Malin Kundang."

"Yes, I remember. Malin Kuntang."

"Kun*dang*. But it is not of hantu in the night. More of a berbicara orang-orang. A people's story of long ago. The kind you learn when you are a child."

"A folk tale. Like Cinderella."

"Like Cinderella. *Yes*. Or, no, there is a better one. Sinbad. The story that one time you told *me*. The story of a sailor. A sailor who arrives from the sea."

He drank the beer and passed the bottle to her and she drank also. She said,

"But if I tell you this story you must not write it down. I would be afraid."

"Afraid?"

"Afraid. When the last story is told and the last story is written, what is to become of the one who tells, the one who writes?"

He wanted to say: We are not the world, we are only ourselves. He received the bottle and smiled across its rim. He said,

"Then we must become more stories, for other people to tell."

and finished the beer and put the empty bottle to his eye like a telescope, describing an arc from the hut in which they lived to the trees that separated them from the sea.

•

The first one handed the binoculars to the second and used the freedom of his hands to lean out over the rail as far as his waist and scan the water immediately below the ship. The semi-automatic slung over his shoulder slid down his arm and clattered against the rail. He muttered *omong kosong!* and let it loose from his hand to lie on the metal deck. The man with the binoculars said,

"Aku bisu melihat negro bajingan."

"Dan Amerika?"

"Jika anda tidak dapat melihat dia dan aku tak bias melihatnya, ia harus mati." He said, "If you can't see him and I can't see him, he must be dead."

"Atau mungkin hantu."

"Hantu, sepasang mereka." He lowered the binoculars and then swung them around so they hung between his shoulder blades. He picked up his own automatic weapon and glanced up at the wheelhouse. The captain was looking down at him, his hair tied back with a red bandanna, a kretek cigarette in an elongated holder jutting like a harpoon from between ivory-white teeth.

The year became a year and a month and the year and a month became a year and a month and a week and the year and a month and a week became a year and a month and a week and a day, and although the girl knew nothing of western philosophy she intuitively understood the principles of Zeno and had simply substituted addition for division to obtain the infinite sequence she so desperately desired. But, of course, she also knew that she was finding foolish solace in a grain of time no bigger than a grain of sand and she had sometimes to stop herself begging the boy with her arms around his knees to not go, not now nor in the smallest division of now, while at the same time noticing that his bare feet made hardly any imprint even where the sand was soft and that when he removed himself from their bed the sheet was nearly as smooth as when the bed had been made. And then, in the hour that followed the day that followed the week that followed the month, she saw him as he came home from the sea, his fishing pole over one shoulder, a string of fish suspended from his other hand, and at the moment he saw her and smiled and held up the morning's catch a shaft of sunlight shone through him and for an extended moment he was as transparent as a sheet of paper held up to the light. And the girl then cried for the whole of the minute that was the minute that followed the hour and did not know that she had fainted until she opened her eyes and saw the lunar craters her tears had made in the hard-packed sandy earth and felt his arms underneath her knees and her shoulders as he lifted her up and felt the breath of his kiss against her cheek and experienced the curiously unreal sensation of being weightless within that which has no weight. She said,

"Thank you, tuan."

and was rewarded with the perfect beauty of his smile as he carried her into the semi-coolness and semi-darkness of the hut.

•

And then one morning, it was very simple, he left the bed they shared and gathered up his fishing pole and walked with an almost imperceptible tread across the hard-packed sandy earth and through the screen of jungle that separated the clearing where their hut was located from the sea . . .

A bird snapped and flapped out of the foliage of the forest, followed almost immediately by the high-pitched raucous shriek of a macaque, and then a small avalanche of minor squawks and chatterings, as of the tumbling of small stones down a mountainside after a car has plunged off the road and somersaulted to silence at the foot of the ravine.

Silence. Only emphasized by a trickle of sand . . .

•

"Please listen."

"I'm listening."

"Pada suatu waktu—"

"Once upon a time—"

"—there was a young man who lived in Sumatra and his name was Malin Kundang. He lived with his sister and his mother and they were very poor. One day a ship arrived from a faraway foreign land—"

"Which land?"

"I do not know, tuan. India? China? A foreign land. And the sailors, they were pirates, they came ashore with many fine things to sell they had stolen, gold and silver and silks and jewels. Many things of more wealth and beauty than these simple fishing people had ever seen. But selling for more money than Malin Kudang, who was *very* poor, could afford to buy. Are you listening?"

"I'm listening."

"It is necessary to listen now. So Malin Kundang, who was previously a boy, became a man. And the man he became became a sailor, became a pirate, a bajak laut, and eventually, after many adventures, became captain of the Sultan's ship. And that was not all, but only the beginning. Because he was very handsome—like yourself, tuan, like Sinbad—and next thing it was true he married the Sultan's daughter. And then he was son of the Sultan—and very nearly a king."

"A pirate king."

"Yes, tuan. A pirate king. But one day and he was far at sea, far from his new land, the Sultan's land, there came a storm and his ship was smashed against the rocks and he nearly drowned, but somehow was washed up upon the shore—"

"I believe this part."

"I believe it also, for it is true. But what happened next? This is where the story becomes more real because more sad. The people in the village by the sea had seen the wreck and came to the beach to receive the shipwrecked captain and his crew. Imagine their amazement when they recognized him and greeted him by his name. Malin Kundang! they cried, Malin Kundang! You have returned to us, Malin Kundang! The members of his crew who had survived looked at him strangely—looked at him and looked at these simple ill-dressed rough-mannered fishing folk who claimed him for their own. And Malin Kundang was angry and ashamed. But before he had a chance to say a word, who should appear but his mother! Yes, tuan, his mother. Ten years older and ten years uglier and ten years more bent than a palm tree in the wind, but he recognized her as immediately as she recognized him, and she said, Malin Kundang, my son, you have come back! And now his anger and shame turned to words, and in front of all the villagers and the handful of his remaining crew he denounced her as a liar, he said: Who are you, you old hag, to call the Sultan's son-in-law your son? And he struck her so she fell to her knees, and this was more terrible because... because—No, just listen, tuan—because she was made to be like a servant or a slave in front of her own people and in front of her son, and the tears ran down her face and Malin Kundang summoned his few remaining men and demanded of the villagers food and shelter and the strongest of their men to help repair his ship. And so they marched through the trees that ran along the shoreline and left Malin Kundang's mother kneeling heartbroken on the sand."

"That is not the end of the story?"

"Why not? It is sad enough and true enough. And is sad enough to be true."

"You cannot leave his mother to weep alone on the sand."

"Why *not?* My *own* mother was the daughter of a penyihir, and died when I was three years old. I think she, too, would have been *jelangkung.* Do not be deceived by tears, my tuan. Now must you hear the story's end?"

"I'm listening."

"Malin Kundang and his men and the villagers repaired the ship. And when it was ready they set sail again for far away lands and the Sultan's palaces and home. And Malin Kundang stood very proud, very Sultan's son-in-law, on the—castle deck?"

"The forward castle. Yes."

"The *for*ward castle, *very* proud. But what came then to the beach except mother of Malin Kudang?"

"Angry?"

"*Very.* Holding boneka fetish, marah dengan kemarahan, and she put a curse on Malin Kudang. And the sky became black and the sea became a sheet of glass and the ship turned into a rock and the sea shattered and the ship and all its sailors, and the Sultan's son-in-law sank down, down to the bottom of the kingdom of the sea."

The face of the girl was yellow and beautiful in the lamplight and the boy sitting up in the bed watched her in semi-profile where she was seated against the unglazed window and studied the way the lamplight played on the angles of her cheekbones and imparted a quality of introspection to her eyes. Then a sudden gust of breeze made the flame of the lamp become tall very suddenly and then snap and flutter and then resume its normal height. She said,

"I think it must be very crowded—in the kingdom of the sea."

•

The arc lamp on the deck of the ship did a final sweep and there was nothing, no more than if a miner had turned the beam of his flashlight on a seam of wet coal. The captain had left the wheelhouse, there was only the Acehnese second mate, his tattoos blue in the lamplight, and he made a sideways movement with the flat of his hand. The sailor in charge of the lamp nodded and brought the apparatus into alignment and flicked the switch that cut off the power. There was a curious echo of the generator after the power had been cut off. The sailor who had been in charge of the lamp took a cigarette out of a battered pack in his shirt pocket, raised it nearly to his mouth, hesitated, then leaned over the rail and spat into the sea.

•

For many nights she sat alone in the hut that was located in a clearing surrounded by trees. During those nights she did not light the lamp and the breeze blew in through the unglazed windows and rustled the sheets of paper that the boy had used to type the stories she had told him through the many previous nights and days. Occasionally she left the hut and walked as far as the trees, but it was many weeks before she walked through them and beyond them to the sea.

The moon was full and very large and the sky was a ceiling painted black and sprinkled with powdered glass. The girl sat on a rock and looked out at the sea. Far away, very far, nearly as far as the horizon, there were the lights of a ship, most likely a container ship bound for Singapore, or maybe further, maybe Manila or Shanghai. And then, by some curious trick of the atmospheric conditions, emphasized / exaggerated by the almost oppressive nearness of the sky, she could hear the echo of voices, as voices echo within the confines of a swimming pool, always louder where you least expect them to be loud, accompanied by everywhere and nowhere ripples of shadow and light. But if, again, from that ship on the far horizon, its lights now fainter as the distance increased, maybe not a container vessel—no!—but a pirate ship, a boy swam ashore, *this* time successfully evading the pitiless sweep of bullets and light, and if the girl waded knee-deep to help the exhausted fugitive through the last few yards of ocean to the shore . . .

Dawn came and the stars faded. And the monitor lizard that made the clearing of the hut safe from rats and snakes, the monitor lizard that had never been seen, turned the rusty key of its tongue in a rusty lock and welcomed with reptilian joy the unforgiving day.

Born in London, **MICHAEL PAUL HOGAN** is a poet, journalist, literary essayist, and fiction writer whose work has appeared extensively in the UK, USA, India, and China. He has published six books of poetry and numerous articles on contemporary literature, photography, and painting in both mainstream and independent magazines. Brought up in England and Wales, he has lived in Key West, India, Sumatra, Java, Thailand, and China, and to support himself during periods of working on experimental poetry and prose has variously sought employment as a commercial fisherman, house painter, bartender, day laborer, radio announcer, and market stall trader. *Artist Descending a Typewriter: 9 Essays on Contemporary Art*, endorsed by Viscountess Bridgeman as "An original and exceptional contribution to contemporary art history," was published by **Shanti Arts** in 2023. *Street Light Bolero* is his first collection of short stories.

**VICTORIA MERKI** (b. 1972, Baku, Azerbaijan) is an artist, illustrator, writer, and publicist. Born into a family of artists, she held her first international exhibition in Berlin at twenty. Since then, her works have been exhibited worldwide—from Europe to the USA and Canada. Merki has illustrated dozens of books and blends philosophy, symbolism, and mysticism in her art. Her paintings, literary essays, and fairy tales weave ancient legends with profound allegories. She currently lives in Germany, continuing to inspire through her work.

www.ingramcontent.com/pod-product-compliance
Lightning Source LLC
Chambersburg PA
CBHW031957010726
47493CB00007B/2236